The day I met Suzie

The day I met Suzie

Chris Higgins

shortlisted
Queen
of teen

Hodder
Children's
Books

A division of
Hachette children's books

First published in Great Britain in 2013
by Hodder Children's Books

1

A Catalogue record for this book is available from the British Library

ISBN 978 0 340 99702 4

Typeset in Berkeley by Avon DataSet Ltd, Bidford-on-Avon, Warwickshire

Printed and bound in Great Britain by
Clays Ltd, St Ives plc

The paper and board used in this paperback by Hodder Children's Books are
natural recyclable products made from wood grown in sustainable forests.
The manufacturing processes conform to the environmental regulations
of the country of origin.

Hodder Children's Books
a division of Hachette Children's Books
338 Euston Road, London NW1 3BH
An Hachette UK company
www.hachette.co.uk

Thanks to:

Tina, for Samaritan advice; Colin, for hairdressing advice; Bill, for legal advice; Naomi, Anne and Lindsey for editorial advice; Twig for all other advice; and Cornish school students for the title.

'Samaritans. Can I help you?'

The voice on the phone is calm, quiet, but it shocks me to the core. Three rings and there she was. She.

I didn't expect to be put straight through.

I can't speak.

I sit hunched in the darkness on the floor beside my bed, clutching the phone to my ear.

I don't know what to say.

I'm a mess.

'You are through to the Samaritans. Can I help?'

I wish you could. A tear rolls down my cheek and I dash it away but more follow. Then my nose starts to run and I sniff and it sounds loud and draggy in the silence of my bedroom.

She'll think I'm disgusting.

'You can talk to me if you want,' she says.

She sounds nice. She sounds like my first teacher in Reception class – what was her name? Mrs Moffat. I loved Mrs Moffat.

I was a good girl then.

I start crying – big ugly sobs that hurt. Once I start, I can't stop.

1

Pulling my knees up I bury my face in my arms, trying to muffle the sound. Everyone is asleep. No one can hear me up here at the top of the house. Except the woman on the end of the phone. She can hear me.

She'll think I'm a nutter.

I don't know how long I cry for. It seems like ages. At last, with big, shuddering gasps, I manage to get myself back under control. I thought I was good at that, controlling things, but I was wrong. I scrub my face angrily. What am I doing? It's nearly two in the morning and I'm ringing a complete stranger.

'I'm still here,' she says softly. 'You can talk to me if you like. When you're ready.'

'I'm so ashamed,' I hear myself whisper. It doesn't sound like me.

'It's OK, I'm listening.'

'I don't know what to do.'

'You can tell me anything you want.'

I shake my head. The silence stretches into eternity. She gives a little cough, like she's trying to remind me she's still there.

At last I say, 'I'll get into trouble if I tell anyone.'

'Don't worry. This is a safe place to talk.'

But I'm scared she's lying. Anger surges through me.

'Yeah, right! I'm not stupid, I know the way you work. Like, if someone was doing something bad to me, you'd have to report them, wouldn't you?'

'No. But I could try to help you.'

'You wouldn't tell on them?' For a moment I feel a flicker of hope, then I realize it must be a trick. My voice turns to scorn. 'What sort of helpline are you? What if I was being bullied or abused or something worse? What if I was being threatened . . . ?' My voice trails away.

'Are you?' she asks, and an image of a dark car with tinted windows flashes across my brain.

'No!' I snap. 'It's not like that!'

Once again she is silent, waiting for me to continue.

After a while I say, uncertainly, 'What if I'm not the victim? Have you thought of that? What if it's me that's done something wrong?'

'I'm not here to judge you,' she says calmly. She's doesn't seem to be the least bit bothered that I yelled at her. Mrs Moffat, dealing with a child in distress. She's not going to be able to stick a plaster on this one and make it better though, is she? The tears start to flow again.

Can I trust her? I don't know who to trust any more. I rock slowly to and fro, moaning to myself, like a crazy person. She'll get fed up of waiting soon. No one likes waiting. Not Scott, not Logan. Nobody.

I hear her voice, far away, indistinct, and put the phone back to my ear.

'What did you say?'

'It sounds like you're having a bad time.'

I feel myself nodding as I choke back the tears.

'Would you like to tell me about it?'

'I can't.'

'Why not?'

'I promised.' My voice is a whisper. 'I promised I wouldn't say anything.'

She waits. I was wrong about her. She's good at waiting. It's like she's got all the time in the world.

'Can you tell me who you promised?' she asks finally.

'My boyfriend. He could get into trouble if he gets caught. He could go to jail.' I moan softly. 'So could I.'

'Anything you tell me is completely confidential.' Her voice is neutral.

I sigh deeply. What have I got to lose? 'I wouldn't know where to begin.'

'At the beginning,' she says. 'In your own words.'

So that's what I do.

I start at the beginning like she says.

The day I met Suzie.

1

It's September, the first day of college. I'm standing in line waiting to register for Hairdressing and Beauty Studies, and I'm about to start the second year. The way I remember it, I'm chatting away to my mate, Mel, who's on the same course as me, catching up on what we did over the summer – which in her case had been lying on a beach in Ibiza in a skimpy bikini and getting trashed, and in my case had been packing in loads of practical experience at Herr Cutz, my work placement, where Gordon, who's as German as I am, kindly took me on for the whole of the summer holidays.

And seeing Rick, of course.

'Lucky!' she says, but I don't ask her if she means getting to hang out with my gorgeous boyfriend or spending weeks on end sweeping up other people's unwanted hair, because I'm distracted by what's going on in front of us. A girl is trying to enrol.

'I can't register you without an address,' says the woman behind the desk emphatically.

'I'll have one soon. I'm seeing a flat this afternoon.'

Her voice is little more than a whisper. No match for Nikki Barton, the cow in the office who thinks she runs the place though everyone knows she only got the job because she's shagging the Principal.

I hate it when weak people get a bit of power and it goes to their heads.

'I need an AD-DRESS,' Nikki repeats, her bright red lips enunciating each syllable slowly like the girl is too thick to understand. She's got lipstick on her teeth. 'I can't enrol you without one. Now please move out of the way.'

The girl, thin and wispy-looking, seems like she's going to cry so I stick my oar in.

'She's staying with me. You can put my address down till she gets one of her own.'

The girl looks up at me, startled, but says nothing. Beside me Mel's giggling as Nikki shoots me a look of pure hatred. But there's nothing she can do. All she needs is an address. Stone-faced, she copies down my address and the girl's details. Her name is Suzie.

Suzie Grey.

'Course?'

For a second the girl looks blank.

'What course do you want to do?' snipes Nikki, like enemy fire.

The girl turns to me. 'What course are *you* doing?'

'Me?' She's startled me. 'Hairdressing. And Beauty. I'm in the second year.'

'Is it all right?'

'Yeah, it's OK. It's good.'

She nods. 'I'll do that one then. Hair and Beauty.'

She turns back to Nikki, who is staring at her by now as if she's grown another head. To be honest she's thrown me too. How random is that? Choose your future by the person standing next to you. I gaze at her back view as she waits for her form to be processed. She's stick-thin, like a starling, I can see her shoulder blades jutting out beneath her top. She's dressed same as us in jeans and a T-shirt but she looks different somehow: drab, mousy and dismal, like she's got the weight of the world on her narrow shoulders.

Mel rolls her eyes and I mouth at her silently behind the girl's back. '*Suzie Grey – suits her!*'

Mel giggles again and the girl turns to stare at her with pale, expressionless eyes. Mel's smile freezes solid on her face. The girl's face is sort of blank but hostile – it's freaky.

Then she looks at me and says, 'Thanks,' before turning away.

'What a weirdo!' gasps Mel, and we watch her walking down the corridor, fair hair hanging limply to her shoulders.

'She looks sad.'

'Is she really living with you?' demands Nikki Barton and I say, 'Yeah, yeah, of course she is.' Though we both know I'm lying.

'Rather you than me!' says Mel as we fill out the papers to enrol on to the second year of Hair and Beauty and then go to find the others in the common room.

Rick isn't there yet. It's a bit early for him. He can sleep for England. But I know he'll haul himself out of bed eventually to re-register on his motor vehicle course because cars are his life and there's nothing else he'd rather be doing. Except seeing me of course.

At least, that's what I thought then.

It's great to catch up with everyone again. I love the first day back after the holidays. The college pools students from miles around and most of them I haven't seen since last term. We're roughly divided into two camps: people like me who've been busy working throughout the summer and people like Mel who've been partying on foreign beaches. Unlike the first, the second camp have wild, wild stories to tell.

'What did you get up to this summer, Ind?' asks Becky, who's on my course too.

'Worked at the salon.'

'All summer?'

'Yeah, it was great. Gordon took me on full-time. I've learned loads. He let me have a go at cutting.'

'Really?' Becky looks impressed. 'I've never done anything other than wash hair and sweep the floor. You're going to be *so* ahead of the rest of us.'

I try not to look smug. I haven't told her the best bit yet. He'd practically promised me a job when I finish college – and jobs like that are like gold-dust at the minute. I decide to keep it to myself.

'Did you see much of Rick?' asks Leah.

'Every night.'

Rick had been working the summer at a garage, cleaning cars and machinery. My boyfriend eats, breathes and sleeps cars. He buys old wrecks and does them up. When he's not at the garage, he can be found under his car of the moment, a Seventies mini, which is his pride and joy. It doesn't really do it for me – though, I must admit, I'd been more than happy for him to ferry me about in it every night. At least with wheels, we could drive out to places and be on our own.

It had been a summer of love . . .

* * *

'Rick?'

'Mmm?'

It was a scorching hot day. Straight after work we'd headed for the coast, desperate to be free of the sticky, airless city and the salon and garage with their cloying smells.

Now we are lying in the sand dunes playing our favourite game. Rick is on his back, face turned towards the evening sun. I'm lying on my stomach directly behind him and I'm stroking a blade of grass gently across his upside-down brow. He can't move, that's the rule. Not a shiver, not a shudder, nothing.

'Why don't you ever invite me to your house?'

I watch his eyebrows drawing together and say, 'You moved!' But he murmurs, 'No I didn't!' and even though he did I carry on, loving being this close to him, studying him. I trail the grass down the frown-line still visible between his eyebrows to the high, straight bridge of his nose, then make a detour across the closed eyelid nearest to me with its thick, black lashes.

I love that contrast of fair hair and dark eyelashes, it's one of the first things I noticed about Rick. 'Answer my question,' I say softly.

'No reason.'

'There must be.' I am so close to him I can feel his breath.

'I want to kiss you,' he moans.

'Not allowed. And anyway, don't change the subject.'

'I'm not. I always want to kiss you.'

'Tell me why you won't take me home and then I'll let you kiss me.'

No answer. He just lies there looking blissed out.

'If you don't tell me I'll go this way.' I draw the grass slowly down his cheekbone and come to rest at the corner of his mouth. It lifts slightly in a torture of anticipation but I let it pass. I'm enjoying this too.

'Nooooo . . .' he groans. 'Not there.'

'Tell me then,' I persist, and when he refuses to answer I begin to trace the outline of his beautiful top lip, the most sensitive part of his face, and it twitches involuntarily.

'Because my dad's a jerk!' he mutters, then he pulls my head towards him. 'Now give me that kiss!'

But it's difficult kissing someone upside down so I wriggle away and stand up, hands on my hips, taunting him. 'You've got to catch me first!'

Rick springs to his feet and I'm off, running towards the sea. He's chasing me and even though I know I'm safe with Rick – he'd never hurt me, he'd never hurt anyone – it's thrilling, like I'm escaping from somebody really dangerous, someone who's out to get me. I scream with excitement on that deserted beach yet at the same time I'm laughing – laughing so much I can hardly stay upright. It's almost a relief when he grabs hold of me at the water's edge and lifts me up into his arms, but I kick anyway like I want to get away.

But now he's threatening to drop me in the sea and I'm fully-dressed and he just might do it – you never know with Rick, he just might – so I really do want to get away now, I'm not pretending any more. I beat his chest and shriek, 'No, Rick! Don't you dare! I'll never speak to you again! I mean it!' The gulls screech in sympathy and in the end he puts me down in shallow water.

'I'm soaked to the skin!' I yell, even though it's not true, only the bottom of my jeans are wet. I kick water, trying to splash him, only he's already soaked through because he's been staggering round in the waves carrying me. All of a sudden, he throws back his head and lets out this almighty roar and suddenly he tears off all his clothes, chucks them on the shore and dives into the waves, coming up shaking his head in a perfect circle of spray.

And that's when I do it. I don't plan this to happen, it just does. I tug off my T-shirt and jeans and my bra and pants and dump them on the sand right next to

Rick's clothes and I dive in too.

It's bloody freezing! I come up beside him gasping with shock. He laughs and pulls me up into his arms and I wrap my arms around his neck and my legs around his hips trying to haul myself up high out of the cold water. But then I look down at his beautiful laughing mouth and I just have to kiss it and it's surprisingly warm and tastes of salt. I dip my head lower to kiss his neck, then his collar-bone, and they taste of salt too.

I search for his mouth again and it's so warm – hot even – his tongue teasing, probing, licking my body into heat like flames in a fire. Overhead the seagulls wheel and squawk. I have never done this before, not in the sea I mean, I don't even know if it's possible. But it is and I gasp again though this time it's not with cold. I'm not cold any more.

It's with surprise.

And delight.

And love.

Afterwards Rick dries me with his T-shirt and then we dress and go to the pub. My clothes are damp and prickly with sand but I don't care. We sit outside under the stars and drink cider and talk and talk and talk. Rick tells me all about his dad, who sounds like a real loser, and his mum, who's perpetually worn out trying to keep things together. We'd been together for ages but this was the first time he'd really off-loaded to me.

'I don't wanna be like him,' he finishes, his beautiful face twisted into a fierce scowl. 'Lazy git. He's never done a decent day's work in his life.'

'You don't have to be,' I tell him. 'What do you want to do?'

'Own my own garage.' His eyes light up. 'I've never told anyone that before. You know something? I didn't even know it myself. But that's what I really want to do.'

'It's a brilliant idea!'

'Yeah.' But then his face falls. 'It's not going to happen though, is it?'

'Why not?'

'People like me don't own their own businesses.'

'Of course they do! I'm going to run my own salon one day!'

He looks at me with a small, twisted smile. 'You're different.'

'No I'm not! Rick, look at me!' I reach up urgently and cup his face in my hands, forcing him to look into my eyes. 'You can be anything you want. You're a brilliant mechanic, you know you are. You just have to plan a bit, save up, work flat out. You can do it, I know you can.'

He stares at me, eyes expressionless, unreadable, and I find myself holding my breath. Watch it, Indigo. You're doing it again. Sorting people's lives out for them. Pushing. You'll push him away if you're not careful.

Then he grins and says, 'I can do it with you by my side. You're the best thing that ever happened to me, Indie,' and he takes me in his arms and we hug like we'll never ever let each other go.

And that was it, we'd set the pattern for the rest of the summer. I don't mean we tore our clothes off every night and rushed into the sea. I just mean that we'd go off together on our own in that little mini and we didn't look for anyone or anything else, we just wanted to be together, the two of us. We fitted, you see. We were enough. And now, maybe, we had a future together . . . I wouldn't have swapped my summer with anyone. It must have showed because Leah sighs.

'You two . . .'

I can't help smiling smugly. Rick is the fittest guy in our year. Tall, fair, blue-eyed and with a smile to die for. Everyone wanted to get off with him at the beginning of college but he chose me. At the Christmas Ball we were voted Hottest Couple of the night.

'You've been together nearly a year now,' says Leah,

who's never had a relationship that lasted more than a week. 'Amazing.'

It *is* amazing, but not in the way that she means. It's amazing because I know that deep down we're so different.

Don't get me wrong, we've got some things in common, obviously. On the surface we're pretty similar, though we don't look alike. He's fair, I'm dark; he's big, I'm small. But we both like having a good time; we both work hard (Rick at cars, me at everything) but manage to have a laugh as well; and we're both (and I'm not being big-headed here) pretty popular on the whole.

Plus we both really fancy each other, obviously.

But underneath, I'm the organized and responsible one, good at managing money and focused on the future. Now I sound boring. Whatever happened to that wild, crazy girl in the sea with her man? But it's true. I know what I want, I know where I'm going, and I'll do whatever it takes to get there.

Whereas Rick is a crazy, live-for-today kind of person who jumps into things without thinking and is hopeless with money. That's why it's so amazing that he's actually thinking about the future for once and wanting to run his own garage.

He'll have a lot to learn though. He is so impulsive,

forever blowing his cash without thinking. Like, for my birthday a few weeks ago he booked a surprise hot-air balloon ride with a champagne picnic. It was awesome, but when I found out how much it cost, I nearly died! We could've had a fortnight in Ibiza for that price.

He blew the money he'd worked so hard for all summer in one go. On me.

They say that opposites attract. Well it's true in our case. He's extravagant, I'm careful; he's impetuous, I'm cautious; he's Mr Good Time Guy, I'm Mother Teresa. He calls me Mother T! I'm the champion of the underdog, the saviour of the lame duck, the patron saint of lost causes.

I can't help it. I'm forever rescuing stray dogs – literally. I once brought home a mad mongrel I found on the street that was chasing its own tail. There was something wrong with it and my dad ended up paying for it to be put down. Then last winter, I found a cat in a black bin liner dumped in a pond. I made Rick rescue it and he was soaked through. And then, when we set it free, it was totally ungrateful! It was completely feral, biting and scratching us to bits.

I should've learned my lesson. Not everyone wants to be saved. But I can't help stepping in if I feel someone needs a hand. Like that girl trying to register. I just had to get involved.

Rick hates it.

What he doesn't get is that he's a bit of a liability himself and that might be part of the attraction – that and the fact that he's drop-dead gorgeous and loves me to bits. I love him too, I really do, but I've got to admit, there's part of me always hopes I can change him. Not all of him, just the bits that get him into trouble. I just wish he'd think before he acts and stop tearing round in cars and spending money like water. Then he'd be perfect.

Anyway, as if I'd conjured him up by thinking about him, my not-quite-perfect boy walks into the common room at that point and immediately I know something is wrong. He's looking really fed up. His eyes are scouring the room, searching for me and, when I wave, he comes straight over and flings himself down next to me.

'Ricky!' squeals Leah and there are high-fives and hugs and kisses all round, but I can tell his heart's not in it. I'm right. When he turns to me, his beautiful blue eyes are dark with rage.

'What's happened?' I ask, and he nods towards the other side of the room where it's quieter and we get to our feet.

'Aahh, they want to be alone,' jeers Mel, and Rick gives her the finger and everyone laughs. But when we sit down, he's not laughing. I take his hand.

'What's up, Rick?'

'I've been done for speeding!' he groans.

And that's how it all began.

I pause for a moment, thinking about how happy I'd been up till that day. The person on the other end of the phone is quiet. I wonder if I've gone on too long. Maybe she's fallen asleep.

'The trouble with happiness, not the crazy-off-your-face-on-something sort, but the normal everyday sort of happiness, is . . . you never know you've got it till it's gone,' I say into the silence. I've thought about this a lot.

'Go on,' she says, like she wants me to explain what I mean.

2

Well, like I said, I'd been fine with working all summer. I love it at the salon, it's like a second home and the people who work there are like my second family. Gordon in particular had been brilliant, teaching me how to cut hair and colour. He's a great tutor and, like Becky said, I know I'm miles ahead of the others on my course. Plus I'd had a good time and he'd paid me for the privilege.

But that night, after Rick had dropped his bombshell, I can't sleep. I'm tossing and turning all night long and all I can think is, I've worked all bloody summer on minimum wage plus a share of the tips while most of my friends were having the time of their lives abroad and now I've got to part with sixty quid of my hard-earned money to pay Rick's fine for him.

Because he's got nothing left, has he? He's blown it all

on me and that bloody balloon flight.

He didn't ask me for it, he wouldn't do that. But the next day, when he comes into college with the weight of the world on his shoulders, I offer. I insist.

'I'm paying it.'

'Don't be daft.'

'I'll have to. You're skint.'

He doesn't deny the fact. He just looks at me with those clear blue eyes of his and says, 'I can't let you do that.'

'Why not? I've got it. I'm flush.'

We both knew it was a lie. I'd saved a bit over the summer because that's the sort of person I am, but my kit and uniform for the second year was going to cost me three or four hundred quid and there were other expenses too. Plus I'd promised myself a new autumn wardrobe.

But he's my boyfriend. I can afford to bail him out, just this once. He's always spending his money on me.

'I'll give it to you at lunchtime. I'll have to get it from the cash machine.'

He kisses me full on the lips, right there in the corridor in front of everyone, which causes a cheer. Then he crushes me to him as if he'll never let me go and whispers, 'Just a loan, right? I'll pay you back.'

'Whatever,' I say, and at that precise moment I honestly

didn't care whether he did or he didn't. It was worth it to see the envy in other girls' eyes. Wrapped in his arms, I spot Sad Suzie from the day before sidling past us. Poor thing. Without thinking, pressed up cosily against Rick's chest, I hear myself saying, 'Did you get your flat sorted?' and, startled, she turns her blank eyes first to me and then to Rick and says, 'Not yet,' before she scurries on.

'Who's that? One of your basket cases?' says Rick, and I punch him in the stomach hard and say, 'Like you, you mean?' and he pretends to double up in pain.

At lunchtime I head off to the cash machine in reception. I've fished my card out of my wallet ready to insert it when someone beats me to it. Unbelievably, it's her. Suzie Grey.

'Sorry!' we say simultaneously and both snatch our hands back and then we laugh.

'After you,' she says.

'No, you go first.'

She slips her card into the machine and I look away while she enters her PIN. But then I hear her sighing heavily and I glance back to see her staring glumly at the amounts and then tapping in ten quid.

'Have you got somewhere to stay?' I ask curiously.

She shrugs. 'I'm all right.'

She doesn't look all right. One of her front teeth is chipped and her hair needs washing. Actually, my experienced eye can tell it needs cutting too, and she's wearing the same clothes as yesterday. Social suicide in this place. She takes the single note from the machine and slips it into her bag.

'All yours.'

I insert my card and tap in my PIN, resisting the urge to cover it over. She's still there and I sense, for all her reticence, she wants to talk. I select my request for cash and I can feel her watching me. When it spits out the wad of notes I pick them up, suddenly embarrassed by my comparative wealth. I find myself saying, as I hold them in my hands, 'It's not for me. It's for my boyfriend.'

Her eyes widen a little.

'It's to pay his fine. Speeding.'

Why was I telling her this? But she nods as if she understood.

'I had a boyfriend like that. Once.'

You had a boyfriend like Rick? I don't think so! But I don't say that, obviously. Instead I say, 'What happened to him?'

'Don't ask.'

I grin as I fold up the notes and stuff them into my back pocket. 'Like that, hey?'

'He was bad news,' she says. 'Seriously bad news.'

I study her for a moment, wondering what he'd done to her. She looks like a victim, with her thin, pale face and straggly hair, the sort of person who gets picked on or beaten up or worse.

I was dying to know what her story was. I can't help it, it's like I've got a magnet in me that attracts me to people like that. Or attracts people like that to me.

People who need my help.

Behind her I could see Rick bearing down on me. He'd spotted me talking to her.

'Got to go,' I say firmly, turning away from her. 'Nice to meet you.'

'You too.'

When I reach Rick, he puts his arm round me. 'Don't even think about it, Mother T!' he warns.

'What?'

'Her.' He jerks his head back towards the girl. 'Your next project.'

'No way!' I say. 'I've got my hands full with you!' I take the money from my pocket and hand it to him. His eyes soften.

'Are you sure?' he says and I say, 'Yes,' and he kisses me.

'Indigo!' We both turn as my name is called.

'What the hell does she want!' groans Rick as I look

back at the girl in surprise. How does she know my name?

She holds up her hand. 'You left your card in the machine.'

I run back to take it from her. 'Thanks.'

'You're welcome.'

'It's nice to know there are still some honest people about.'

'Honest, but skint.' She gives me a fleeting smile and just for a brief second she looks almost pretty. I glance back at Rick.

'Look, do you want a coffee later?'

She looks surprised, then pleased, then confused, like she wants to but she can't because she's broke.

'My treat,' I say quickly. 'For finding my card. I owe you.'

'OK.' This time she smiles properly and I'm right, she is pretty, behind that frightened mask.

'Right then,' I say. 'See you in the coffee bar at four.'

3

I get there early but she's already waiting for me. I order us some coffees and say, 'Do you want anything to eat?' and she goes, 'No, it's OK,' but I can see her eyes lingering on the cakes.

'Sod it,' I say. 'I'm going to have some carrot cake so you'll have to as well or I'll look like a greedy pig.'

But it was her that was the greedy pig. When we sat down, she wolfed down her cake like there was no tomorrow.

Afterwards she knocks back her cappuccino, then she sits back in her chair and sighs deeply.

'Thanks for that. I was starving.'

I stare at her. 'Have you eaten today?'

She frowns. 'I had some biscuits this morning.'

'Are you anorexic?'

'Does it look like it?' she says sharply, licking the icing off her fingers.

'Not exactly.' She looks like she could be, but the way she stuffed the cake down herself tells me different.

'Well then. If you must know, I'm a bit short of cash at the moment.'

'You took some money out at lunchtime,' I point out and she darts me a look as if to say, what's it to do with you? 'Sorry, none of my business.'

'It's all right. I know you're trying to help but you can't. The fact is, I need that money for a bed tonight.'

'Ten quid for a bed? Where are you staying? Not the Ritz, I'm guessing.'

'The hostel down Dock Street. It's only temporary,' she adds defensively.

Dock Street is a dive. I could imagine what the hostel was like.

No I couldn't. I've never been in one.

'Not living at home then?'

Her jaw drops and she blinks her eyes once, like I'm stupid.

'Duh! Obviously not.'

Her whole tone said, Stay away from me, Pinocchio, but I couldn't help it, I had to keep going. If you saw her, you would've too. She was trying to be tough but she was too little and scruffy and pathetic to fool anyone.

'Where's home?'

'I haven't got one.'

'Everyone's got a home.'

'Shows how much you know.' Her voice has a bitter edge to it. After a while she says, 'I was with someone but I've left him.'

'Why?'

'You're one nosy cow!' But then she adds, 'Because he was a shit, if you must know.'

He beat her up, I knew he did. She had that look about her.

'You did the right thing leaving him then,' I say, like I knew anything about it, and she must've thought the same because she gives a short, sharp yelp of a laugh.

'You reckon? Well, you're probably right, but now I've got nowhere to live and nothing to live on.'

'You can get help, here at college. They can find you somewhere to live, help you get benefits. If you go to the office—'

'Ask that slapper for help? No thanks.'

'No, they've got to, it's the law . . .'

'Yeah, but the problem is, to get that sort of aid I've got to give them loads of information.'

'So?'

31

She looks at me as if I'm missing something.

'You don't get it, do you? I don't want him to find me. I don't want him to know where I am.'

It's more serious than I thought. I haven't got a clue what goes on, me, living at home with my mum and dad, going about my nice, uneventful, organized life.

Suddenly she jumps to her feet. 'I've got to go. Make sure I've got a bed for the night. Thanks for the coffee and cake.'

'Look, if you need anything . . .'

'Do you want that cake?' She looks at the slice of carrot cake I'd hardly started because I'd been so busy talking to her.

'Help yourself.'

She finishes it off in a few big gulps.

'If you need anything else . . .'

'Like what? A place to live? A job? Three meals a day?'

Surprised by her bluntness, I find myself lost for words. 'Anything . . .'

'Yeah, thanks.' She's dismissive and I don't blame her. It's the sort of pointless phrase people say all the time but don't mean, like *Have a nice day* or *Let's go for a drink sometime* or *See you later*.

The difference was, I meant it. But she didn't know that.

I want to at least give her some money to buy dinner.

As she walks away I call out urgently, 'Suzie?'

She turns round and says, 'Yeah?' and her face is sort of hopeful. But then I remember, too late, I've given all my money to Rick.

'See you tomorrow,' I say lamely and she sighs.

'Yeah, see you.'

I watch her walking away and I feel so sorry for her – and sort of outraged on her behalf. She's only a skinny little kid, no matter how tough she pretends to be. No one should be hungry in this country in the twenty-first century; everyone has a right to a bed to sleep in.

How naïve was I?

Now I know there are worse things than being hungry and homeless.

Far worse.

I feel myself filling up again.

I can't speak any more.

'Can you tell me what happened to Suzie?'

The voice in my ear is like a lifeline. I don't know how long I've been here adrift in the darkness, alone with my thoughts.

But I'm not alone, am I? She's still there at the other end of the line.

I hear my voice, stark and grim, like it belongs to someone else.

'Suzie disappeared.'

4

She didn't disappear straight away. In fact, she gradually became more and more visible over the next few weeks. She was always there floating about on my radar, never very far away, much to my friends' amusement and Rick's annoyance. I'd bump into her in the Hair and Beauty block, not surprising since she'd signed up for the course, or I'd be in the common room with Rick and a gang of mates and there she'd be.

'She's stalking us!' grumbles Rick and I laugh.

'Don't be daft. You just notice her because she's always on her own and she's a bit . . .'

'Weird.'

'No – different.'

It was odd though, the way she'd suddenly appeared from nowhere and become part of our lives. Bizarrely, because she was so inconspicuous, I'd notice if she wasn't there, if you know what I mean. She was kind of spooky, like an apparition drifting around the edge of my life. Yet she stuck out like a sore thumb.

'There's your friend,' remarks Mel one day towards the end of a blow-drying class. I was being the stylist, she was my client. I look up to see Suzie coming quietly into the college salon, like a wraith. 'She looks like she could do with a makeover herself.'

'She's not my friend,' I mutter, then I add, 'Hi, Suzie! How's it going?'

'Good,' she says, though she could've fooled me. She looked as drab and woebegone as ever, her hard little face in sharp contrast to the rest of the pretty, bubbly, wannabe hairdressers in the department.

'Found somewhere to live?'

'Not yet.' She wanders over and watches me teasing Mel's hair into shape. 'Looks nice.'

'Thanks.' Mel's tone is uninviting. Strange how one polite, insignificant little word can convey such dislike.

'Who cuts it for you?'

'She does.' Mel indicates me in the mirror and then, to my surprise, Suzie says, 'Will you do mine for me?'

'I only do friends,' I say, without thinking. Mel snorts in amusement as Suzie's face darkens and, too late, I realize what I've said. 'I mean . . .'

'It's all right.' She turns away.

I look to Mel for help, but she's too busy sniggering so I yell, 'Suzie! Wait!' and she turns back, expressionless. 'I didn't mean it like that. I meant, I'm only just learning, I can't charge people . . .'

'Suits me,' she says. 'When can you fit me in?'

'Freeloader!' says Mel under her breath.

How the hell do I get out of this? Suzie's face is stiff with resentment. She knows I'm going to make an excuse. I'm going to let her down, like everyone else does. I hear myself saying, 'Tomorrow? After college?'

'Fine.'

'Your place or mine?' I ask, trying to lighten things up a bit but she doesn't smile.

'What do *you* think?'

'Mine it is then. See you about seven. Do you know where it is?'

'I'll find it.'

She looks Mel up and down insolently before she turns away.

In the mirror I can see my friend's eyes widening, then she shudders.

'She is one freaky bitch!'

'She's just a bit of a loser.'

39

'She's got you wrapped round her little finger!'

'She won't turn up, she was just messing about. She doesn't even know where I live.'

'She does you know. You gave her your address to register at college.'

Mel could tell by the expression on my face I'd forgotten that momentarily. She looks so smug I laugh out loud.

'I'm just doing the girl a favour and cutting her hair, that's all. You said yourself she could do with a makeover.'

'Well, watch your back, that's all I'm saying.'

I laughed at Mel that day.

The way she was going on, you'd have thought I was the victim, not Suzie.

5

The next day she turns up at my house on the dot of seven in the pouring rain. My sister, Tamsyn, had come round for dinner and we'd just sat down at the table when the doorbell went.

'Who on earth can that be on a night like this?' asks Mum. 'Are you expecting anyone?'

'No,' Tamsyn and I answer together. Dad doesn't bother, he's too busy tucking into his roast beef, plus a ring at the front door is never for him anyway. I had totally forgotten about my offer to cut Suzie's hair for her, not surprising since technically I *hadn't* offered. Anyway, no one is more surprised than me when Mum leads Suzie Grey into the room.

'Someone to see you, Indigo,' she says.

Suzie looks more bedraggled than usual, if that's

possible. Her wet hair is hanging down in dripping rats'
tails over the collar of her thin jacket, which is soaked
through. She is literally shivering with cold.

'Let me take your coat,' says Mum. 'You're drenched.'
She helps Suzie peel off her jacket and eyes her doubtfully.
'We're just having dinner. Would you like to join us?'

Suzie's eyes dart to the food on the table and an
expression of longing flickers over her face.

'No, thanks,' she says. 'You carry on. I'll wait.' She
perches at the far end of the sofa, sniffing mournfully, and
I try to continue with my meal but it's difficult with
someone sitting metres away from me, cold, wet and
obviously hungry. Regretfully, I put my knife and fork
down with my plate still full.

'I've finished,' I say, and Mum doesn't object as
she normally would but just says quietly, 'It'll keep
till later.'

'Coming, Suzie?' I ask, and she gets up at once like a
little dog and trots after me obediently.

When I reach the narrow stairs on the first floor that
lead up to my room, I glance back and am amused to
catch her sneaking a look into a bedroom as she passes.
'This way,' I say and, though she knows I've caught her
out, she doesn't look embarrassed, she just scrambles up
the stairs after me to the top floor. I open my bedroom

42

door and stand aside to let her enter and am gratified to hear a gasp.

'This is so cool! Is it all yours?'

'Yep,' I say with satisfaction. 'All of it.'

She walks to the centre of the room and looks around in astonishment. I have to say, my bedroom *is* pretty awesome. It takes up the whole of the roof space and the ceiling is sloped where the beams come down to the floor. My dad built it especially for me.

Along one side of the room is a long, wide worktop which doubles as a desk, laden with college files plus my lap-top, a television and an iPod. A computer chair slots beneath it and above it are shelves stacked with books and photos and bits and pieces. Next to it is an en-suite shower room.

On the other side of the room my bed, piled high with pillows and cushions, is in the far corner, tucked away comfortably underneath the eaves. Beside it, there's a chest of drawers and a standard lamp which, when I flick it on, casts a welcoming pool of yellow light on to the polished wooden floorboards. You can see it reflected in the three large velux windows in the roof.

In the opposite corner there's a built-in wardrobe and apart from that there's a bookcase overflowing with yet more books, a rocking chair with a throw over it, a stand-alone mirror, a couple of brightly-coloured rugs and that's it. As well as heaps of clothes, make-up, magazines and hair stuff, of course.

You'd love my room, everyone does. It's pretty special. But no one ever loved it as much as Suzie.

'I can't imagine having this much space to myself!' she says, her eyes alight. She really meant it, I could tell, she was so impressed.

'Did you have to share a bedroom when you were little?' I ask.

'Yeah!' She frowns as if it's a daft question. 'I shared a bedroom all my life.'

'It must be nice to come from a big family,' I say, to make her feel better. 'I've only got one sister. I wouldn't mind having more – or some brothers . . .' I can feel myself starting to rabbit on as if I'm the one who's ill at ease, even though it's my room, my house.

'Is that your sister – downstairs?'

'Yeah, that's Tamsyn.'

'Where does she sleep?'

'She doesn't. She used to have a bedroom on the first floor but she lives with her boyfriend now. She's just come over for dinner.'

She nods and stares around the room again, drinking it all in.

'Have *you* got a sister?'

She shakes her head.

'Brothers?'

'Nah. I've got no one, me. I'm on my own.'

So who did she share a bedroom with then? Mel's right, this girl is weird. 'What about your parents?' I ask.

She throws the question back at me, challenging. 'What about them?'

'Well, where are they? Why don't you live with them?'

Her eyebrows rise and immediately I feel uncomfortable. 'Sorry,' I say. 'I didn't mean to pry.'

She shrugs. 'It's no big deal. I haven't got any. None that matter, anyway. I've been in care most of my life.'

So that explained it. The bedroom-sharing. Plus the air of loneliness that surrounds her like a rotten smell.

'Not everyone is as lucky as you,' she adds, flopping down on my bed. She reaches for the framed photo of Rick on the chest of drawers. 'How long have you two been together?'

'Nearly a year.'

She studies the photo closely and says, so quietly I'm not sure I heard it right, 'You've got it all, haven't you?'

What are you supposed to say to that? I stand there awkwardly in the centre of *my* room while she lolls on *my* bed, staring at a photo of *my* boyfriend. I've never met anyone quite like her before. She is such an unnerving mixture of pathetic-pushy, hesitant-hostile, mousy-malevolent. No, not malevolent, that makes her sound evil. But there is a touch of passive-aggressive about her. You don't know where you are with her from one minute to the next.

Mel's words of warning flood through my mind. '*Watch your back, that's all I'm saying.*'

That's when I reached over and took the scissors from the shelf.

Silence.

I've stopped talking at last.

The person at the other end of the phone is still listening, I can tell. But something has changed. I can feel the tension.

'What did you do with the scissors?'

'What?'

'Would you like to tell me what you did with the scissors?'

I'm silent as I try to work out what she's getting at.

Then I laugh uncertainly.

'What do you think I did with them? Stabbed her?'

Her voice is the same, quiet, well-modulated. 'I don't think anything. I'm just here to listen.'

But she's lying. I know that's what she thought, that I'd stuck the scissors into Suzie, and now I can feel myself getting angry.

'What sort of person do you think I am? A bloody MURDERER!'

'I am just trying to understand what happened.'

'Then LISTEN! I'm trying to tell you, you stupid cow!'

I am so incensed, I think I'll burst. After all I'd done for Suzie, this idiot on the end of the phone thinks I'd stabbed her in the back!

I drop the phone from my hand like it's contaminated and bend over, hugging my anger to me like a physical pain. Then I lose it. A howl of anguish drags itself up from somewhere deep inside me and I raise my head and stare up through the velux window at the night sky. The moon has moved into view. I'm a mad dog, baying at the moon. But mad dogs don't cry real tears.

At last my sobs subside. I've done it now. She's gone. My one lifeline on the darkest night of my life and I've driven her away.

I pick the phone up. 'I'm sorry! I didn't mean it!'

'That's OK.'

I feel weak with relief. She's still there. She's waiting for me.

'I'm not like that. I don't call people names.'

'You're upset.' Her voice is so kind, it makes me start to cry again.

'I don't know what to call you,' I sob.

'Do you want to know my name?'

'I know it already,' I say. 'It's Mrs Moffat.'

Silence.

Now she'll be totally convinced I am mad.

When I started school at four and a bit and my teacher said her name was Mrs Moffat, I was so pleased because I thought she'd said Miss Muffet, like in the nursery rhyme. I knew it off by heart.

Little Miss Muffet

Sat on a tuffet

Eating her curds and whey.

There came a big spider, who sat down beside her

And frightened Miss Muffet away.

I'll have frightened this woman away now.

But then she chuckles and I do too, only mine is more of a choking yelp of relief that she still hasn't given up on me.

'You can call me that if you want.' She pauses. 'Would you like to tell me your name?'

I pause. Can I trust her? I picture Mrs Moffat with her kind, round face and her soft, squashy bosom that I would use any excuse to fold myself into. I hear myself saying, just as I did that first day at school, 'I'm Indigo. But everyone calls me Indie.'

'Indie,' she repeats. 'Do you want to tell me what happened next?'

'I wanted to help,' I say. 'So I cut Suzie's hair for her.'

6

'How do you want it?' I ask.

'Like yours.'

'Are you serious?'

'Absolutely.' Suzie gives me that intense stare I'm starting to recognize. 'I love it. I want to look like that.'

'I don't know.' I lift her limp hair and examine it doubtfully. 'It's finer than mine. I don't know whether it would work.'

'Just do it,' she says, so I set to.

I take her into the en-suite first and wash her still-damp hair in the hand-basin with my best shampoo. I give her a head massage at the same time, like I've been trained to do. Beneath my fingertips, I can feel her relaxing. Then I condition and treat it, using various

51

posh products from the salon which Gordon let me have at cost price.

Her hair wrapped in a clean towel, I lead her back into my bedroom and sit her down on the computer chair in front of the mirror. In all this time, she's not said a word.

I place a dry towel around her neck with a flourish. 'Tea, coffee, madam?' I say as a joke and am surprised when she takes me seriously and answers, 'Coffee please.'

'Later,' I say and comb her hair through. I hesitate. 'Like mine?' I check, and she nods so without another word I make a start. Her decision, not mine.

As I lift sections of her hair with my comb and start chopping them into shape I have this weird thought that in a way she reminds me of Rick, though he wouldn't thank me for saying so. They share the same kind of reckless, impulsive streak. *Do it. NOW.* But I have to say Rick wins outright on the personality front. Poor Suzie has had a bit of a bypass there. It's impossible to know what she's thinking.

Initially I feel a bit nervous cutting her hair but then I get a grip, reckoning she can always tell me to stop if she doesn't like what I'm doing. But she stares at her reflection impassively and just lets me get on with it. I work away at her hair, combing it, lifting it, snipping it, fingering it into shape and all the time she watches.

At last, I lay down the scissors. I'm finished.

'What do you think?'

'All right. Can't tell till it's dry.'

I can feel myself bristling as I pick up the hair-dryer and my styling brush. Is that all the thanks I get? I'm doing this as a favour, remember? But I want her to like it so I take my time drying it as carefully as I can, even adding some expensive mousse to give it body.

Finally it's done.

'Well?'

If she doesn't like it I'll tell her to get lost. I've spent ages on this and saved her a small fortune. But her eyes light up and she turns her head from side to side, preening, a huge smile on her face.

'OMG! I *love* it!'

I have to admit, it does suit her. It brings out the best of her features. Now her face is no longer hidden behind a curtain of lank hair, you can see she's got good cheekbones, a small, straight nose and a cute, determined chin. But best of all are her eyes. They look huge now you can see them properly, striking even, lit up for once with pleasure.

She's transformed.

'Look!' she says. 'Put your face next to mine.' I bend down and do as she says. 'I look like you now,' she says triumphantly.

I study our faces in the mirror.

Her hair is fair, mine is dark.

My eyes are hazel, hers are a washed-out blue.

One of her front teeth is chipped, mine are perfect.

My skin is olive, hers is fair.

She has freckles, I don't.

I have a mole on my right cheek, she doesn't.

Her brows need plucking, mine are shaped to perfection.

But, the shape of the head, the line of the neck, the curve of the cheek, the form of the eyes, nose, chin – why hadn't I noticed it before?

She's right.

We do look alike.

7

'Can I have that coffee now?' Suzie says once she's finished admiring herself, and I'm struck by her cheek, but I switch some music on for her then go downstairs to make her one anyway. I *had* offered after all, even though it was supposed to be a joke. I notice my dinner still waiting for me on the table and my stomach rumbles with longing. There's no sign of Mum and Dad but Tamsyn glances up from the sofa, where she's curled up reading a magazine and sipping tea.

'Where's Orphan Annie?' she remarks.

'Upstairs,' I say, filling the kettle. Then I add for good measure, 'Actually her name's Suzie, but you're right, she is an orphan.'

Tam, in mid-gulp, splutters and spits back tea into her mug. 'Really?' she says. 'Sorry! I was only joking. Poor kid.'

I'm so pleased with the effect my words have had on my sister that I push away the guilty thought that I don't know if this is technically true. Suzie had told me she had no family and had been brought up in care, but I wasn't sure if her parents were dead or just not interested. Anyway, it had wiped the smug smile off Tamsyn's face.

'I've cut her hair for her.'

'What's it look like?'

'Better.'

'That wouldn't be hard. You giving her a makeover?'

'I wasn't planning to.' I glance again at my abandoned meal.

'I will then.' She grabs her bag from the floor beside her and says, 'I'm going to give your friend a make-up lesson.'

'She's not my friend!' I protest but it's too late, Tam is already moving quickly and soundlessly up the stairs. I shove the plate into the microwave and set the timer for three minutes. That should be enough. Hopefully Tamsyn will stay up there with my strange guest long enough for me to eat dinner.

But as the microwave pings and I turn around with the plate in my hands, she's appeared again, frowning.

'Where did you come from?'

'She's going through your stuff.'

'What do you mean?'

'That girl. In your bedroom. She was looking through all your things. She didn't see me. She had her back to me.'

'So?' I stare at my sister in surprise. 'No harm in looking, is there?'

'It wasn't like that. She was pulling things off the shelves, examining them.'

'What? Private stuff?'

'I dunno. Books and things. Photos.'

'Was she going through the drawers?'

'No.'

So why was she making such a fuss? Doesn't everyone look at other people's books and photographs? What was wrong with that?

But I'd noticed something about Suzie. People were wary of her – no, it was more than that, they took against her, even though I was convinced she was harmless. First Nikki Barton, though she takes against everyone unless their face fits. But then Mel and Rick and now Tamsyn. What was it about pathetic little Suzie Grey that put people's backs up?

She needed someone on her side, there was no doubt about it. I put down my plate with a regretful sigh and made two coffees instead, trying to remember if she took sugar. I knew nothing about Suzie but she'd waltzed – no that was the wrong word, she'd *drifted* into my life and somehow, probably because nobody else would, nobody else cared enough, I felt responsible for her.

If she needed a friend – which clearly she did – then it looked as if it was going to have to be me. I stir in a spoonful of sugar just in case and stare at Tamsyn icily.

'*You* are making a fuss about nothing. Now if you'll excuse me, I'm going to take my *friend* a drink if that's all right with you.'

I sail upstairs sanctimoniously, my nose in the air, carrying a mug of coffee in each hand. Behind me I hear Tamsyn intone, in a deep, hollow voice like she's got a part in some B horror movie, 'YOU'LL BE SORRY!' She knows she's overreacted and is now hamming it up to make me laugh, but I ignore her.

When I arrive at my bedroom door, Suzie is there to greet me. She takes a mug from me, sits down in the rocking chair and takes a sip.

'Anything to go with this?'

'Pardon?'

'Biscuit or something?'

No please or thank you. I'm trying to be her friend but she's not making it easy.

'Didn't anyone ever tell you it's rude to ask?'

Her smile fades. 'If you don't ask, you don't get.' She sips her coffee moodily, rocking herself to and fro. Then she says, 'You want me to go, don't you?'

'I've got some work to do,' I admit. 'I expect you have too.'

She pulls a face. 'Can't get any work done in that place. It's too noisy. People coming and going all the time.'

'You need to move into somewhere better. I can help if you want?'

'How?'

'I can look in the paper for you. Or online. Find somewhere cheap.'

'I've got somewhere cheap.'

'Somewhere better than that. A studio flat or a room in a shared house.'

She snorts. 'You've got no idea, have you? Places like that, they want deposits, references . . .'

I don't ask her why she hasn't got any references. I don't need to. Someone like her – well, she wouldn't, would she? Especially if she was on the run from some guy. She'd probably done a midnight flit, leaving everything, including her debts, behind her.

She was right. I had no idea.

I get up and go over to my bag and take out my wallet. 'Look, I'm sorry, it's not much because I gave most of it to Rick. But I can let you have a bit of cash to help you get by.' I thrust a couple of fivers into her hand.

I don't know what I expected. Maybe that she'd weep with gratitude? Or she'd fling her arms around my neck and be eternally grateful, like Rick? Anyway, I was wrong. She stands up, her small face enraged.

'I don't want your money. I'm not a charity case, you know.'

'I know that—'

'You think I'm on the scrounge, don't you? Just because I asked you to cut my hair for me. Just because I asked you for a bleeding biscuit!'

I stare at her, open-mouthed. Where did all this anger come from?

'I didn't mean to offend you—'

'No, your sort never do. Bloody do-gooders. Get off on it, do you? Makes you feel better about yourself? Giving your miserly hand-outs to the poor and needy.'

'Don't be like that!'

'Don't be like what – ungrateful? For that?' She chucks the notes at my feet, her face contorted with anger. 'You can go to hell! I can get more than that anytime I want.'

She jumps up and grabs her coat.

'Suzie! I didn't mean—'

Tugging a purse from her pocket, she opens it and

shakes it upside down. Coins tumble out to make a bid for freedom on the floorboards.

'That's for the coffee,' she spits. '*And*, by the way, I don't take sugar.'

'Sorry—'

'I'll get you the money for the haircut as soon as I can.'

'I don't want it!'

'Tough!' As she turns to go I see the hurt on her face and her final words wound me more than all the venom that has gone before.

'I thought you were my friend,' she says.

'Is that the last you saw of her?' prompts the voice at the end of the line.

'No. I saw her the very next day.'

Then she ignored me when I tried to talk to her. I'd collected up all the coins I could find off the floor to give back to her. It only came to one pound twenty-seven – not even enough for a cup of coffee. That's all she had in her purse. But when I went up and offered them to her in the canteen the next day, she looked right through me like I was invisible and turned away. Mel was with me and she stared first at me and then at Suzie's rigid back as I took my place in the lunch queue, my cheeks burning.

8

'Is that . . . ?'

'Suzie Grey.'

'She's had her hair cut.'

'I know.'

'It's like yours.'

'I know.'

'Did you do it?'

'Yes.'

'Doesn't she like it?'

'Yes, she does actually.'

'Only she seems a bit upset.'

'I know. I've upset her.'

'How?'

'What is this, twenty questions? I offered her money.'

'What for?'

'To help her out.'

'Is that all?'

'She was offended. I hurt her feelings. I shouldn't have done it.'

Mel laughs and puts her arm around me. 'She is one weird, mixed-up kid. Forget about her. She's not your problem.'

I know Mel's right. But as we sit down at a table nearby and our mates join us and our table grows noisier and noisier, I can't help being aware of Suzie as she sits silently by herself, nursing a mug of tea.

I keep thinking: Whose problem is she if she's not mine? But I know the answer already.

She's nobody's problem. She's on her own.

My problem comes along then, Rick, and soon some of his mates join us. He's full of a new car someone has told him about. I mean new car as in old-car-but-new-to-him. Like I said, my boyfriend thinks his sole purpose on earth is to do up old bangers. I'm kind of half listening and half keeping an eye on sad Suzie when I realize with a shock that the way Rick is talking to his mates, he sounds like he's planning to buy this car.

'Um, excuse me.' I sit up straight, interrupting him mid-flow. 'Just exactly how do you propose to do that?'

'Whoa! Watch out, Rick, she's on the case!' whoops

Dan, and Rick laughs good-naturedly.

'You haven't got any money,' I remind him, in front of everyone.

Rick's grin slips. 'OOOH!' says Mel. 'TROUBLE IN PARADISE!' and everyone laughs. Her voice is so loud people at other tables glance over, including Suzie.

I'm being harsh I know, but I really have to end this here and now because I know what Rick's like. Once it takes root in his brain he'll stop at nothing till he gets what he wants. But now his mate Dan starts making clucking noises and flapping his arms about like a chicken to imply Rick is hen-pecked and the rest of the boys join in. Rick starts to look annoyed.

'And you've already got a car,' I point out.

'I can trade it in for the new one,' he says. 'It's a little beauty, an early-sixties Triumph Herald convertible. They're really rare nowadays. It's got a—'

'RI-ICK!' My voice with its warning note comes out louder than I intended and everything goes quiet. Suzie lifts her head up to see what's going on. I know I sound like Rick's mum, but I can't stop. 'You CAN'T buy a new car.'

'Don't tell me what I can and can't do,' he snaps, his eyes ablaze. Everyone is looking at us.

He's forgotten, I know he has. He's fallen completely in

love with this Triumph Whatever and everything else has gone right out of his head. It's like going out with a serial adulterer, only the objects of his affections have bodies made of metal, not flesh. He can't wait to get dirty again under another old bonnet. And he's totally forgotten he still owes me sixty quid for his speeding fine.

Short of reminding him of this in front of everyone, which he won't thank me for, there's not a lot else I can say. Sometimes I could strangle him!

'Do what the hell you want!'

I get up and stalk out of the canteen. Behind me I hear a muted cheer from the boys, quickly hushed up by the girls. As I pass Suzie I see her gazing up at me. She looks like she wants to say something but I brush past her before she's got the chance.

Stuff her. Stuff Rick. Stuff the lot of them.

I'd had it with trying to help people.

I stop talking, remembering how angry I'd felt that day.

Mrs Moffat waits for a while then she says, 'I can see that you felt your help was not appreciated by Suzie and you were being taken for granted by Rick.'

'Too bloody right I did!'

'Did you stick to your decision and refuse to help them any more?'

'Huh!' Hot, dry anger flares up inside me again. It's almost a welcome relief from the tide of despair I've been engulfed in recently. 'I wish! If I had I wouldn't be in this mess.'

'Go on.'

'I didn't hear from Rick. I didn't expect to. I knew he'd be stewing for a while because I'd made him look small in front of his mates. Plus, he would still be obsessing about that crappy car. I didn't care, I was mad at him. I didn't want to see him. He was a bloody liability.

'My phone was unusually quiet that evening. Mel had rung to find out what was going on between us but she started saying she thought I'd been a bit harsh on Rick so I told her to keep her nose out of it. She didn't know about the money I'd lent him and I wasn't about to tell her. She must've passed the message around that I was still in a bad mood because no one else rang. My anger drained away and I started to feel sorry for myself. Why bother with anyone? Nobody cared about me.

'I felt really low that night.'

'Did you feel suicidal?'

I practically jump clean out of my skin. 'No, course not!' I snap at the voice at the end of the phone. 'I told you, I was just feeling sorry for myself.'

Mrs Moffat lapses back into silence. Then I wish I hadn't been so quick to react. Because the truth is, there have been times since when I thought I couldn't go on, when I wanted to end it all. But not then. Looking at what happened later, this bit was easy.

But she didn't know that. How could she unless I told her?

So I carry on explaining.

9

After a while, Mum calls up to tell me I've got a visitor. I automatically assume it's my errant boyfriend, come to apologize. Despite myself, hearing feet on the stairs, I dash a brush through my hair and dab on some lippy.

But disappointingly, it's Suzie Grey who appears in the doorway of my room.

'What do you want?' I say in surprise.

'I've come to see if you're OK?'

'I'm fine.'

She looks different. It's the haircut, it's got to be, because nothing else has changed. She's still wearing the same drab clothes. But her new short, cropped hairstyle really suits her. It makes her look more confident. She's looking at me straight in the face, instead of peering at me nervously from behind a wispy curtain of hair.

71

'You didn't look fine at lunchtime.'

Her voice is different too. Full of concern. She could be Mel.

'Have you fallen out with your boyfriend?'

'I would've thought that was blatantly obvious.'

'What did you row about?'

'It's none of your business.'

'Was it about the money?'

I stare at her in surprise. How did she know? But then I remember she's the only person who *could* know. She was the sole person I'd told that I'd lent money to Rick to pay his fine.

'I heard what you said in the canteen. He wants to buy a car. What a tosser!'

I find myself bristling. 'Do you mind? That's my boyfriend you're talking about!'

'Well he is. He owes you money but he still wants a new car.'

She's getting feisty. But part of me can't help feeling vindicated as she sums it up so neatly in so few words. That part of me which had started to feel mean and small-minded for being angry with Rick for forgetting that he owed me money.

She pulls a twenty-pound note from her pocket and hands it to me.

'What's this for?'

'The haircut.'

'I don't want it.'

'Take it. It's yours. *I* pay my debts.'

I take the note from her fingers, ignoring the sanctimonious tone in her voice. 'Where did you get it?'

'Never you mind.' Her face darkens. 'I didn't nick it, if that's what you mean!'

'I didn't mean that. You can't afford it.'

'How do you know? And anyway, I told you, I don't want your charity.'

'It's not charity. It was a freebie. A one-off.'

I hold the note out to her but she refuses to accept it, her face pinched and cross, like a fierce little ferret.

'I'm not a scrounger.'

'I know you're not. It was a gift.'

'I don't accept gifts.'

'From one friend to another.'

Her face softens.

'Take it.'

'Are you really my friend?'

'I said I was, didn't I?'

Her hand comes out, reluctantly.

'Are you sure?'

'Of course I'm sure. Idiot!'

She smiles at me then and tucks the money into her pocket.

'It looks great by the way. Really suits you.'

'I know.' She picks up my lippy off the desk. 'Mind if I try this on?'

She is so weird! One minute she's telling me she's not a scrounger, the next she's stealing my make-up. But then I realize that is what Mel and Becky and Leah and I do all the time, try each other's stuff. It's what friends do.

And I've just told her she's my friend. So now she thinks she can do it too.

There is definitely something odd about her. Like, she doesn't really get the fact that you have to know someone properly before you start using their things. But as I watch her applying lippy (badly!) I find her strangely endearing. She's like a little kid who hasn't quite learned how to act in the world. That's why she comes across as peculiar.

I knew why. I'd done Sociology for GCSE. It was because of her dysfunctional childhood.

She needed socializing. She needed someone like me to take her in hand.

'Give it to me,' I say, taking the lippy gently from her fingers. 'I'll do it for you.'

I end up giving her the works. A complete makeover. I

can't do much with her nails because they're bitten down to the quick, but I pluck her eyebrows into shape. By the time I've finished, she looks gorgeous.

She looks like me.

I'm not being funny or big-headed or anything, but honest to God, with that haircut and make-up, she really did look like me. Me at my best, I have to say, like when I'm going on a big night out. I suppose it's not that surprising really, because not only does the make-up belong to me, but I'm the one who's putting it on her, in exactly the same way as I do my own face. Her eyes, outlined in smokey-grey, look enormous. It's funny how before I thought they were a bit odd. Now I think they're her best feature.

'You look stunning,' I say.

'Thanks.' Then she adds, 'So do you. You always look good.'

We stand, side by side, staring at ourselves in the mirror. The similarity is striking.

'We're like twins!' she laughs and I do too and then we look even more alike.

'Different colouring,' I point out.

'And different clothes.' She glances down at her old jeans and top and pulls a face. She's not half so pretty when she's serious.

'You need to practise smiling a bit,' I suggest.

'Never had much to smile about,' she says morosely.

On impulse, I open my wardrobe and start rifling through its contents.

'I need to sort mine out. Are these any good to you? They'd only be going to . . .' Just in time I stop myself from saying the word *charity* and substitute '. . . *recycling*. You could save me a trip.'

I pull out stuff and fling it on to the bed. Her eyes light up and she starts picking through it, trying things on. She's like a kid let loose in a sweet shop.

It all looks good on her, I have to say. I've got an eye for clothes, everyone says so. I know what suits me and it suits her too, maybe even more so because she's skinnier than me. By the time she's finished, she's sorted herself quite a bundle: jeans, tops, jumper or two, duffle coat, bag, even a pair of ankle boots.

'D'you want something for these?' she asks, pulling the twenty-pound note back out of her pocket.

I laugh. 'Put it away. I told you, you're doing me a favour!'

'Are you sure?'

'Positive.'

'You're too bloody soft for your own good, you are,' she says, shaking her head, but she can't stuff them into the bag quick enough, as if she's afraid I'll change my mind.

Not long afterwards she leaves, wearing the coat and boots, bag over her arm.

Then Rick turns up. Weirdly, he looks surprised to see me.

'What are you doing here?'

'Um? Oh yeah, it's my bedroom. Could that have anything to do with it?'

He shakes his head. 'I could've sworn I just saw you disappearing round the corner. You had your navy blue coat on with the hood up . . .'

He stands in the doorway looking puzzled and I have to laugh to myself. Suzie dressed in my clothes, no wonder he was confused. But instead of enlightening him I say, 'More to the point, what are *you* doing in my bedroom? Especially if you thought I wasn't here?'

'I asked your mum if I could leave this for you.' He hands me a posh store bag.

'I don't want it,' I say rudely, but it's pretty obvious I don't mean it because I can't resist peeking inside. There, nestling provocatively on a bed of white tissue paper in its distinctive silver-and-gold bottle is my favourite perfume.

'To say sorry,' he says simply, and I fling my arms around his neck.

'It's too much! You shouldn't have!' I say, and though I'm thrilled that he did, I can't help wondering where on earth he got the money from.

'You're worth it.'

'You shouted at me in front of everyone!' I say, trying not to let him off too easily.

'You told me off in front of everyone!' he responds then immediately adds, 'Sorry! I'm sorry. I'm an idiot.'

'Yes, you are,' I say. But I'm in his arms and his lips stop my protests and all my best intentions go awry as my insides turn to jelly.

That's the thing about being in love with Rick. It's horrible when we fall out, but it's brilliant making up afterwards.

'So you and Rick are in love?' asks Mrs Moffat.

I pause for a while, remembering how crazy I was about him then.

'Yes. No. I don't know. I thought I was but now I'm not so sure. I'm not sure of anything any more.'

'What did he do to make you feel differently about him?'

'Well, for a start, he bought the bloody car!'

He didn't tell me straight away. In fact he didn't tell me at all.

10

I'm sitting outside college a few days later, enjoying the September sun. It's lunchtime and there's quite a crowd of us: Mel and me, of course, Leah and Becky, Dan, Will, Toby and a few others. Suzie has joined us too. I don't think Mel is exactly thrilled about this – she seems to have really taken against Suzie. Well, she can stuff it. Suzie's not doing anyone any harm. In company she reverts to being a quiet little thing, though already I know there's a lot more to her than meets the eye.

There's no sign of Rick, though. Then suddenly, this funny little two-tone, open-topped car drives in through the gates.

'Sound!' Dan, who is sprawling on the grass nearby, jumps to his feet. Immediately Will follows him and, by the time the car comes to a halt in front of me, it's surrounded by salivating boys.

'What is it with boys and their toys?' I say in my most superior voice.

Mel laughs. 'You've taken it well, I must say.'

Too late, I see that it's Rick behind the driving wheel. I don't believe it at first. *How could he? He'd promised me!* But then I realize he hadn't promised me a thing. I'd just assumed because he'd come round all-repentant, bearing gifts and wanting to make up, that he'd seen sense and kicked all thought of this flaming car into touch.

I should've known better. That perfume wasn't a gift. It was a bribe. And I'd fallen for it.

I could feel the girls looking at me, waiting for me to explode. Well, I wasn't going to give them the satisfaction. I stand up and saunter slowly down to the car where Rick is in the driving seat and they follow me. Rick looks up at me apprehensively and bizarrely I'm reminded of that scene from *Grease*, where Danny meets Sandy. Boys surrounding him, girls behind me, and he's got that same daft expression on his face as John Travolta does in the film. Half love-sick dog for me; half bad-boy attitude for his mates.

'What do you think, babe?' he says, and even his words sound like they come from a high-school musical. I take a look at the car and I honestly can't see what the fuss is about. It's small, with two doors and a big windscreen and it looks like a tin-can on wheels, one of those funny little cans of sardines with sharp edges. At least, I conclude with relief, it couldn't have cost him much.

'Wanna take a ride?' he asks. I can't believe it. Consciously or not, he is acting like some relic from an old American movie. I tug open the door, which is sticking a bit, and slip in beside him.

'Take it away!' I drawl, deciding to save face by playing along with him for now, and he grins widely as he turns the key in the ignition and starts up the engine.

Only it doesn't start. It growls and chokes and splutters and wheezes, like an old man clearing his throat.

Then it dies.

Everyone laughs.

Rick's face falls. 'Needs a bit of work on it,' he explains needlessly. 'I knew that. That's why I got it for a good price.'

'I thought you didn't have any money,' I say between gritted teeth, but he ignores me as everyone piles behind to bump-start us down the drive. We jerk our way out through the gate to the sound of cheering and applause.

As we pick up speed and head for the centre of town, Rick relaxes visibly beside me. He leans his elbow out of the open window and rests his right hand lightly on the steering wheel, and his pride of ownership in the car is almost tangible. Then he rests his left hand on my knee like he owns me too.

'Sweet,' he says, his voice rich with self-satisfaction. I don't know if he's referring to me or the car but I brush his hand away in irritation.

'Nice little runner,' he remarks after a while.

Then, 'Engine's sounding good now.'

I sit there, refusing to respond to his trite comments, getting more and more angry by the minute. The wind is whipping my hair all over the place and it's hard to have a conversation above the noise of the engine. After a while he tries the more direct approach.

'What do you think of it then?'

'How much did it cost?'

Annoyance flits across Rick's face. 'Not a lot.'

'Where did you get the money from?'

'I traded in the mini for it.'

'Straight swap, was it?'

He's silent. Looks even more annoyed, if that's possible. His foot presses down on the accelerator and the car surges forward in a wave of noise.

'I asked you a question,' I remind him. 'Did you swap the one for the other?'

'Not exactly.'

'What does that mean?'

'The guy was great. He said I could pay off the difference later on.'

'Later on *when*?'

'Whenever! What's it to you? Each month, if you must know.'

'Each month for how long?'

'I don't know!' His voice rises.

'*You don't know?*' Mine rises even higher.

'Two years.'

'*Two years!*' Now I'm practically screaming.

'Stop repeating everything I say like a bloody parrot! It's fine. It's under control. I'll be working full-time next year.'

'So what about *this* year?'

'I can handle it. I've got my Saturday job. It's enough.'

'Rick – it's *not* enough . . .'

'It is. Stop keeping on, you're doing my head in. It's got nothing to do with you!'

'Yes it has!' I say, stung to the core. 'It's got everything to do with me. You still owe me money.'

'You'll get your effing money! You know that!'

'When? I've been waiting long enough!'

'Now! You can have it right now. Anything to stop your bloody nagging!'

The rest of his words are lost in a squeal of brakes as he suddenly twists the steering wheel and does a U-turn into the opposite lane of traffic. I grab hold of the door to keep myself upright.

'What are you doing?' I yell.

'Cash machine,' he says grimly, swerving to miss a van which blasts its horn at us. I shriek with fright as Rick struggles for control of the car. But then the wail of a police siren drowns me out.

'Shit!' Rick's face pales and I know even before he bangs his foot down on the accelerator that he's going to make a bolt for it.

'DON'T!' I scream at him. 'Don't do it, Rick! It's not worth it. Just stop. You're in enough trouble already!'

'Did the police catch him?' Mrs Moffat asks, as I struggle to regain my composure.

'Yeah. There was no car chase. He did as I asked and waited for them. He had to go to court. We thought they were going to do him for dangerous driving at first and that was mega-serious. He could've gone to prison for that. But because no one got hurt and he co-operated with the police, he got done for driving without due care and attention and 'cause he pleaded guilty he got off with three penalty points and a fine.'

'Not too bad then?'

'Huh! The fine was bad enough, five hundred pounds. But it was worse than that. What we didn't know then was, if you've been driving for less than two years and you get six points or more as a new driver, you automatically lose your licence. That was a real tragedy for him.

'See, the thing was, Rick had to drive, it was part of his job. I don't just mean his Saturday job, I'm talking about his future. It messed up everything. When he left college he wanted to be a motor mechanic and no one would take him on if he couldn't drive.'

'So he would have to apply for a provisional licence and do his test all over again?'

'Yep. And you know how expensive that is.'

'That must have been hard for him?'

Mrs Moffat, whoever you are, you are so easy to talk to. It's like talking to a friend. Only any friend of mine would've been far more judgemental.

'It was. Cars were Rick's life.' Then I add in a small voice, 'It was hard for me too. It was all my fault, you see.'

'Why?'

'He wouldn't have turned the car round in the first place if it wasn't for me going on about the money he owed me. Sixty quid, that's all! And even then he might have got away with it if he'd put his foot down – but I was the one who made him stay and face up to it. It was all down to me, you see.'

'So Rick blamed you for what happened?' she asks.

'No,' I say softly. 'He never did that, not once. It was me. I blamed myself.'

11

I couldn't look at Rick that day in the magistrate's court when they told him they were taking his licence away. I'd made him do the right thing – and look what had happened. I felt like I'd let him down. So what did I do? I let him down even more. I ran off and left him on his own.

I thought he'd ring me, but he didn't. I wandered round in a daze for a while and eventually ended up at college. I was due a practical assessment that afternoon, but when I got there I was late and I knew I wouldn't be able to get my head around it anyway so I went along to the café instead. My mates were all in class but Suzie was there on her own, nursing an empty mug as usual. I sank down into a seat next to her and she looked up.

'What's wrong?' she asks.

I shake my head. She doesn't keep on, she just gets to her feet and goes and buys me a cup of tea without asking, even though I know she hasn't got two pennies to rub together. Then she sits back down and it all comes out, the lot of it.

She turns out to be a good listener, Suzie. She doesn't interrupt or offer an opinion about Rick for once, she just lets me get on with it. The only thing she does is gasp when she hears how much his fine is.

'How's he going to pay that?' she asks, and I shrug my shoulders.

'I haven't a clue.'

Afterwards, she walks me back to my place and ends up staying for dinner. She does all the talking, thank goodness, mainly about college, and I can see Mum and Dad warming to her. I didn't know she could be so sociable.

Later on we go upstairs and she says, 'My turn this time,' and gives me a massage, a proper Indian head massage, the full works – head, face, neck and shoulders. It's the most relaxing thing in the world. 'Good for relieving stress,' she says, and she's right. I can feel myself calming down.

'You done this before?' I murmur.

'Nope. But I've watched people do it.'

'You're a quick learner.'

'I am, aren't I?' She sounds pleased.

And then, maybe because she's so good at it or maybe because I'm so wiped out by everything, I curl up on my bed and fall asleep.

When I wake up it's pitch dark and the luminous numbers on my alarm clock show me it's almost midnight. As my eyes adjust to the darkness, I see the outline of a person sitting totally still in the rocking chair and I shriek with fear.

'Shh!' Suzie's voice is quiet and reassuring. 'It's only me.'

'What are you still doing here?' I ask, my heart thudding.

'Didn't want to leave you, the state you were in.'

'Has Rick phoned?' I struggle to sit up, but she says 'No.' I pull my phone out from my bag and check it anyway, but there's nothing and I'm so sad. She must know because she comes across and puts her arm around me.

'Don't worry about him, he's not worth it.'

We sit there together in the darkness and I feel sorry for myself and wonder if she's right. I'm glad she's with me.

'D'you want me to stay the night?' she asks. Without thinking I say 'Yes,' because I'm feeling so lonely without Rick, and I know that's what she wants me to say, and anyway, it's not fair to expect her to go home on her own at this time of night. Especially to Dock Street. So I get out my sleeping bag and make up a bed for her on the floor. And she looks really happy snuggling down inside it, like a kid on a sleepover. Don't suppose you have too many of those when you're brought up in care.

'Don't forget to turn your phone off,' she says sleepily. 'I hate being disturbed.' And I do as I'm told because, let's face it, Rick is not going to ring me at this time of night if he hasn't rung me up till now. He'll be off his face somewhere with his mates.

And then I lie awake all night long, worrying that I've been dumped.

I suppose I must have dropped off in the end because the light is filtering through my curtains when Mum taps on my bedroom door with one of those, 'What's going on?' looks on her face. Rick's at the front door wanting to speak to me.

By the time I'm out of the bathroom, where I've tried to repair the damage a sleepless night has done to my face, Suzie is already downstairs, eating cornflakes and chatting away happily to Mum and Dad at the kitchen table. Rick sits mutely opposite her, looking really pissed off. From the look of him I guess he didn't get too much sleep either.

It's pretty obvious he wants to talk to me privately, but Suzie doesn't seem to pick up on it at all. We end up, the three of us, walking to college together, hardly saying a word.

When we get there Rick pulls me to one side and finally Suzie takes the hint. But even then, before she leaves us alone, she lays her hand on my arm and says, 'I'm here if you need me, yeah? See you later.'

'What is she, your keeper?' he says, scowling at her back view. There is blatantly no love lost between these two.

'Leave her alone, she's been nice to me. She knows I'm upset.'

'*You're* upset! Why aren't you speaking to me?'

'I am!'

'Well, you weren't last night.'

'You didn't ring me.'

'Yes I did!'

'When?'

'All bloody night!'

I stare at him in surprise. 'No you didn't.'

'I did! You wouldn't answer your phone. I left messages for you.' He looks raw, like I've really hurt him.

'I fell asleep. And then when I woke up, I turned it off.' I pull out my phone and switch it back on. He's right. Messages and unanswered calls appear one after the other. 'I'm sorry!' But then I frown. 'You can't blame me, Rick. You didn't ring me till after midnight.'

'I did! I rang you right through the evening. Once I'd calmed down . . .' He looks a bit sheepish.

'Well, there's nothing on here – look!' One of us is telling lies and it's not me. He couldn't have rung while I was asleep because Suzie would've said and there was no record of unanswered calls. I bet he'd gone out drowning his sorrows with his mates, then had an attack of conscience when he got home.

'But I did! Look!' He starts clicking through his mobile like he's got a point to prove, but I take it from his hand. It's not important.

'Forget it. You're here now, that's all that matters.'

He puts his arms round me and I gaze up at him.

'I'm sorry,' he says, and I can tell he means it.

'So am I.'

'What have you got to be sorry for?'

'Going on about the money. Not letting you get away when you had the chance.'

'I'd have been in deeper shit if I'd got into a car chase.'

'Running off like that when you were in court . . .'

'Why did you do that?'

'I thought you'd hate me.'

'I could never hate you.'

'It was all my fault . . .'

'No, it was my fault. I'm an idiot . . .'

'*I'm* an idiot . . .'

His lips crush mine and we stop arguing.

We go to our morning lessons but then bunk off for the rest of the day. D'you know where we go? Rick's car. The heap of metal that started all the trouble in the first place. Well, it's private even if it's not very romantic. No one can see us in his garage. I've never actually set foot inside Rick's house, I think he might be ashamed of it. Idiot. I don't care what it's like. But we're probably safer in the garage.

I'm just glad we're still together.

Afterwards, Rick walks me back home, his arm enclosing me like he'll never let me go.

'I've never felt like this about anyone before,' he says.

'Nor me.'

It was true. It seemed to be the more problems life threw at us, the stronger our relationship became. We had a lot to work out. Rick had a massive fine to pay, plus the cost and time implications of doing his test all over again, but we'd manage, somehow, between us.

We had to. No one else was going to come to our aid. Rick's parents had their own problems and I certainly wasn't going to ask mine for help. Their opinion of Rick was low enough as it was.

'I'm going to help you sort this,' I say.

'Good.' Then he stops and looks down at me. 'But let's keep it to ourselves, yeah? No one else needs to know.'

I nod, wondering whether I should confess to him that I'd already confided in Suzie. Suzie, of all people – he couldn't stand her! But she wouldn't say anything if I asked her not to. Let's face it, she had no one to tell anyway.

It would be bound to come out eventually, though. My heart sank. It would probably be in the weekly paper and then my dad would have something to say about it.

'Don't look so serious. If we can survive this, we can survive anything,' he says with that irresistible grin of his. Then he bends his head and seals his words with a kiss.

I believed him. I really did. I truly believed that life could only get better. That's what love does to you.

But then we carry on walking and turn the corner into my street and Rick stops short. 'What the hell . . . ?'

I'll never forget the look on his face. Kind of bemused and incredulous, like he couldn't quite believe what he was seeing.

Suzie was sitting on my garden wall waiting for me.

12

She's wearing jeans and the top I'd lent her that morning because she didn't have anything clean with her and the ankle boots I'd already passed on to her. The bag that used to be mine is on the ground beside her. She's reading something and her head is bent so her face is hidden behind the sweep of hair that I'd cut into my style.

The hair that she has now dyed dark brown, exactly the same shade as mine.

'She's copied you,' states Rick flatly. 'She's a bloody clone.'

He's got a point. It could be me sitting there. It's like staring at a photo of myself.

Suzie looks up and smiles. 'What d'you think?' Her face is alight as she waits for an answer.

What do I think? Well, I don't think sad victim any

more, that's for sure. She's lost that look completely. She's more dirty, sexy grunge.

Is that what I look like?

'Do you like it? I did it myself. This afternoon.'

Her smile fades a little and she looks uncertain. The old Suzie creeping back to the surface. Poor kid. Her self-esteem is only skin-deep. I try to find something positive to say.

'It's great. It alters you completely. It makes you look—'

'Like you.' Rick glares first at her and then at me as if it's my fault. Then he mutters, 'What the hell is she trying to do?'

'Rick,' I say warningly but then, to my horror, he adds more loudly, 'I've got one girlfriend. I don't need two.'

'Shut up! This isn't about you!' I hiss, but it's too late, I'm sure Suzie's heard what he said because she darts him a look of pure venom. But then it's gone, quick as a flash, and I think I might have imagined it.

'Better be getting on,' she says, sliding off the wall. 'See you tomorrow.'

'Did you want anything?' I ask as she walks away.

'Nah!' She turns round and gives me that blank stare of hers. 'Just wanted to see you were all right.'

'I'm fine.'

'I can see that,' she says and walks off down the road.

'I like your hair!' I call after her. Beside me, Rick snorts. She lifts an arm and waves, but doesn't turn back.

When she's disappeared round the corner Rick says, 'That is one weird cow. You want to stay away from her, Indie.'

'Why? She's harmless.'

He shakes his head. 'She's nuts! Always hanging around, wanting to be with you, wanting to *be* you.'

'She doesn't know anyone else.'

'She's wearing your clothes, didn't you notice? She's doing her hair like you. She's copying you.'

'That's what friends do.'

'When they're kids. Not when they're your age.'

'She hasn't got anyone else to model herself on, has she? Anyway, it's not her fault. I gave her those clothes, remember? She doesn't have anything else to wear.'

'That's what all girls say – *I've got nothing to wear!*' His voice, high and girly, makes me want to slap him. 'It doesn't mean you've got to dress them up in your clothes. She's not a bleeding doll, Indie.'

'It's not like that!' I say, stung to the quick. 'She's a really sad case, Rick. She's got nothing. No one. She's on her own.'

'You and your Mother Teresa act.' He shakes his head. 'She's like a bloody leech, sucking you dry.'

His face is earnest. This is *so* unlike him. He's normally so laid-back he's horizontal.

Rick really did not like Suzie.

'Drama Queen!' I laugh, but underneath I've got to admit, I'm spooked too.

It's not just that she's copying me. I can't help wondering whether she deleted those phone calls from Rick when I was asleep. I wouldn't put it past her.

To be honest, she was starting to get on my nerves too.

A polite cough reminds me someone is still there at the end of the phone. I hear her voice, slightly hesitant now.

'You told me earlier that Suzie disappeared. Can you tell me a bit more about this?'

'What?'

'You said before that she'd disappeared.'

I laugh.

'It was just a figure of speech, that's all. I didn't mean she'd been abducted or something.'

And then it hits me like a brick wall.

Rick really didn't like Suzie, I'd said. Mrs Moffat thought he'd done something to her!

'Rick didn't do away with Suzie, if that's what you're getting at!' My angry voice rings out in the dark, silent house. Mum and Dad are sleeping one floor beneath me. Careful, Indie, if you start shouting, you could wake them up.

'Rick is not like that, you idiot!' I hiss down the phone. 'He wouldn't harm a fly!'

Silence. I shouldn't have called her an idiot. She'll hang up on me now.

So what? She doesn't understand a thing I'm telling her.

103

She just jumps to conclusions.

'You're not paying attention. There's no point in talking to you. You're not listening to a word I say.'

I sound like a spoiled brat. But underneath, a terrified little voice is whispering, Don't go. Please don't leave me. I need you, Mrs Moffat. I need you to help me.

'I am listening, Indie,' *she says.* 'I'm just trying to follow everything you've been telling me.'

'Well try a bit harder then! You've got it all wrong.' *I'm so rude, I would hang up on me.*

But she doesn't. Instead she says, her voice even as usual, 'OK. Would you mind clarifying a point for me? When exactly did Suzie vanish?'

I groan and butt my forehead against the wall, the pain almost a welcome relief to the turmoil going on inside me. 'I didn't mean it like that.'

I take a deep breath.

'When I said Suzie disappeared, I wasn't talking about her going missing like some kid on Crimewatch. What I meant was, Suzie Grey gradually faded away like an old photograph.

'And Scarlett took her place.'

13

When she walks into the common room the day after she dyed her hair, most people react like Rick did.

Leah's jaw drops open a metre.

'OMG! Indie! Have you seen that?'

'There's two of you!' squeals Becky.

'What a freak!' breathes Mel. 'She looks just like you!'

'Thanks!'

'You know what I mean. It's like she's deliberately modelled herself on you . . .'

'Don't you start!' I sigh. 'I've had it up to here with Rick. She freaks him out too.'

'You'd think he'd be pleased,' says Becky, giggling. 'It's every guy's dream. A nice cosy threesome . . .'

'Do you mind?' I protest as everyone laughs. Suzie

glances over at the noise and sees us all gawping at her. 'Actually,' I continue, trying to put a stop to their merriment, 'you couldn't be further from the truth. Rick can't stand her.'

'Don't blame him,' says Mel. '*That* is spooky.'

'Watch out, she's coming this way!' shrieks Leah, grabbing a newspaper and pretending to be engrossed. But the illusion is spoiled by her shoulders shaking up and down.

'Don't laugh! Don't laugh!' mutters Mel.

'Hi, Suzie,' trills Becky. 'Nice hair.'

'Thanks.' Suzie slips into the seat beside me and looks at the others suspiciously.

'Like Indigo's,' smirks Becky.

'Just like Indigo's,' sniggers Mel.

'*Exactly* like Indigo's,' yelps Leah from behind the paper and the three of them fall about screeching like hyenas.

'Just ignore them,' I say, trying not to laugh myself. 'They can't help it, poor things.'

Suzie shrugs but I can tell they're getting to her. A pulse is beating in her neck that I've never noticed before. Inadvertently I touch my own neck at the same spot. Have I got one there too?

Of course I have. We're all the same under the skin. Aren't we?

'Do you have a problem?' Suzie is looking straight at Mel.

Mel sits bolt upright. 'Do *I* have a problem?' she repeats. 'It's not *me* with the problem, hon.'

'Leave her alone,' I say quietly, but Suzie stands her ground.

'Have I upset you in some way? Because if I have, I'm sorry. I didn't mean to.'

'Huh?' Mel's eyebrows disappear into her fringe. 'It's not me you need to apologize to. It's Indie.'

'Why?' Suzie turns to me, looking upset. 'What have I done?'

'Nothing.'

Mel clears her throat. 'Excuse me?'

'Leave it, Mel,' I say warningly.

'No I won't. She doesn't get it, so maybe someone had better put her straight.'

'Tell me what?'

Mel leans over the table and pushes her face up close to Suzie's.

'Watch my lips. Stop jumping on Indie's bandwagon. Stop queering her pitch. Get out of her face.'

'What do you mean?'

Suzie looks startled, like she genuinely doesn't understand what Mel is on about.

Mel rolls her eyes. 'Let me spell it out for you.' She starts ticking off on her fingers. 'One – the course you signed up for. Same as Indie's. Two – the clothes. Same as Indie's.'

'She gave them to me!'

Mel ignores her. 'Three – the make-up. Same as Indie's. Four – the haircut. Same as Indie's. Five – the colour. Same as Indie's . . . What next, Suzie Grey? A boob job? Nose job? Personality transplant?'

Mel's hard voice rings out throughout the common room. People look up and giggle and then the room falls silent. Becky and Leah begin to look uncomfortable but Mel, in the limelight, won't let it go.

'Tell me, what part of COPYCAT don't you understand?'

Suzie jumps to her feet and stares at me with huge, sad eyes. She looks like a whipped puppy dog, one that doesn't know what it's done wrong.

'I'm sorry,' she says in a broken voice. 'I didn't mean it. I was only trying to fit in.'

Then she runs from the room. People start talking again amongst themselves.

I glare at Mel.

'*That*,' I say, 'was cruel.'

Then I run after Suzie.

14

I search high and low for her, eventually tracking her down in the girls' toilets. She's locked herself inside a cubicle and I can hear her sniffing. When I knock on the door and say, 'Suzie? Is that you in there?' she doesn't reply, so I know it's her. I settle down to wait. In the end she comes out, her eyes red and sore-looking.

'You've been crying,' I say unnecessarily, and she shrugs. She looks so forlorn, standing there, like she doesn't know what to do.

'Wash your face in cold water,' I suggest. 'It'll make you feel better.' She turns on the tap obediently. It's like talking to a child.

'Take no notice of Mel, she's just a gobby cow.'

She scoops water up and splashes her face. I hand her a paper towel and she takes it from me without a word.

When she's finished scrubbing her face dry she leans forward, her hands on the washbasin, and stares at herself gloomily in the mirror.

'What a state!' she says, her eyes full of self-loathing. 'Why are you wasting your time on a loser like me?'

'You're not a loser.'

'Yes I am. Look at me.'

Her nose is red, her eyes puffy, her expression hopeless. You can almost smell the despair coming off her in clammy waves. I have to force myself not to turn away.

'Your friend's right,' she says. 'I copied you. Your hair, your look, everything.'

I study her sad reflection and hope I don't look like her.

'Why?' I ask.

'I wanted to be like you.'

I lay my hand on her arm. 'Just be yourself.'

She shakes it off irritably. 'Why? Who would want to be me? No one in their right mind.'

'You don't mean that . . .'

'Don't I? What would you know about it?' She screws the paper towel into a ball and chucks it in the bin, turning to face me, her voice bitter. 'You with your posh house and your fancy bedroom . . . your family who looks after you . . . your mates who stand up for you . . . plus a boyfriend who worships the ground you walk on! How could you understand what it's like to be me?'

I stand there feeling helpless.

'I can't,' I say. 'Unless you tell me.'

I learned from Suzie that day in the toilets what a cosy, cushioned life I'd led, one which I had simply taken for granted. Things that I just assumed I had a right to, I found out were actually a privilege. Things like a roof over my head, food on the table, a clean, warm bed to sleep in at night. A mum and dad who cared about me, a sister who looked out for me, friends who included me, a boyfriend who was fun and kind and treated me right. I had a life. I had a future. I had a place in the world.

Not like Suzie. I knew she'd been brought up in the care system. I knew she'd run away from her boyfriend because he hadn't treated her right. I knew life was tough for her, but I had no idea how tough it really was. You see, I believed she still had choices. I presumed she was in control of her life, like I was.

How wrong could you be?

She told me everything, right there in the ladies, her back against a washbasin, her arms folded across her thin body like a shield. Whenever I smell disinfectant, I associate it with Suzie's pinched little face that day as she poured out to me her horrendous story.

No father. An alcoholic mother who left her on her own, or worse still, with random 'aunts' and 'uncles', while she disappeared for days on end. Poor kid, she was doomed from the start. Eventually her mother had abandoned her completely and little Suzie Grey was consigned to care.

'Funny word that,' she sniffs. '*Care*. What does that mean to you?'

'I don't know,' I say, struggling to understand. 'A place of safety? Somewhere where you're looked after, protected, loved?'

'Yeah, right!' Her expression is bitter. 'Shows how much you know.'

I'm sure for some people it is like that. But not for Suzie. Care for her was a place where she learned to never trust a soul. It was her misfortune to come across all sorts of damaged people on both sides of the care system, clients and so-called 'carers'. You don't want to know what happened to her in some of the places she ended up in.

'I went from one home to the next,' she says emptily. 'They were all crap. I was in and out of foster homes too.

Some of them were all right. But then my mum would turn up out of the blue and claim me back, full of promises. Then things would go wrong and I'd be dumped back into care again, wherever they could find a place that would take me.'

Suzie's life was a nightmare. A childhood of neglect followed by an adolescence of abuse. I guess it was inevitable with a background like hers that when she left the care system she'd fall straight into an exploitative relationship and confuse it with love. What would she know? She suffered violence at the hands of some smack-addict.

'He used and abused me,' she says, but I don't want to repeat what he made her do, just to get money to fuel his dirty drug-habit. One day, when she'd resisted, he punched her in the face, breaking her nose and cracking her teeth, and she'd ended up in hospital.

'That's when I left him,' she explains. 'I did a bunk from hospital. Escaped from his clutches and came down here. I'm free now.'

But she's not free. She lives in terror that one day he'll catch up with her.

There's more to her story than that. Loads more.

I couldn't take it in, it was so awful.

She recounts it all to me in a monotone with that awful

blank look on her face and in the end I find myself sobbing with the horror of it all. And she's the one who stretches out her arms to comfort me.

'It's all right,' she says, patting me on the back. 'It's over now. I'm never going back to him.'

'But how will you manage?' I moan. 'You need help. We'll go to the authorities . . .'

'No!' She pushes me away, her face fierce. 'I told you! I never want to see him again. If I go through the system he can trace me. He'll send his mates after me. You don't know what he's like.'

'But you've got no money. You need food, clothes, books and things. You need to find somewhere decent to live.'

'I've got somewhere to live . . .'

'For how long? You've got no money coming in. How long can you afford to pay for that dump?'

'Mind your own business!'

I wish I could. But I can't.

'You can't stay in hiding forever, Suzie! You need to sign on, claim benefits . . .'

'I can manage, I told you! I have up to now, haven't I?' Her face is tense, angry, drawn. 'Anyone can get money if they have to. I can do stuff . . .'

Her voice trails away. She doesn't say any more.

She doesn't need to. Conversation over. She bends down and picks up her bag from the floor, the one that used to belong to me.

Gently, I take it from her hand with its raw, bitten nails.

'Come on,' I sigh. 'You're coming home with me.'

'So you took Suzie into your own home?' asks Mrs Moffat.

'Yeah. I found her a job as well.'

Even now I can hear the pride in my own voice.

But everyone knows pride comes before a fall.

'That was good of you,' she says. 'I expect she was grateful.'

'Grateful?' I think about it. 'Yeah, I suppose she was. In her own way.'

Gratitude was something I never associated with Suzie. Like she said, what did she have to be grateful for?

15

Mum and Dad were both OK with Suzie staying at our place for a while. They've always been good like that: not fussy or house-proud or bothered about the extra face at breakfast. I was always the one people came to for sleepovers when I was at school.

Though I must admit, Rick has never stayed over, not once. They've never said he couldn't, but then, I've never asked. I think I was probably afraid my dad would have a fit. Like my sister says, if you don't want to know the answer, don't ask the question.

You see, I know my dad's not that enamoured with my choice of boyfriend. He's never come right out and said so, but I can tell. It's more what he doesn't say, than what he does. I've seen him pulling a face at Mum if Rick's running a bit late or voicing an opinion he doesn't agree with or going on and on about cars or making himself too much at home. I know Dad thinks he's not good enough for me. He's not clever enough. He's a rev-head. He's from the wrong side of town.

I'm not saying Rick's perfect. I'm not saying he doesn't have faults. What Dad doesn't realize is that I love Rick and I know how to handle him.

Or I thought I did.

Tamsyn said not to worry, he was just the same with her. But he wasn't. Tam had moved out to live with her boyfriend, Dave, last year and he'd hardly turned a hair. But then Dave was an accountant in a suit which, if it's not exactly on a par with neurosurgery, is definitely a few notches up from a mechanic in oily overalls.

The strange thing was, Dad was perfectly OK with Suzie moving in with us. But Tam didn't like it one bit. When she next came round to find Suzie installed upstairs, she went ballistic!

'What is that weird girl doing in my room?' she screeched.

'Shh! She'll hear you!'

'Has she moved in?'

'Just for a bit. Till she gets on her feet.'

'You don't know the first thing about her!'

'Yes I do. I know she's got no family and nowhere to live.'

'That's not your problem.'

'No, it's hers. But I can help. Anyway, it's no skin off your nose.'

'Yes it is! She's sleeping in my bedroom!'

'It's not your bedroom any more,' I point out. 'You sleep with Dave, remember? Dave and his briefcase.'

'Mu-um! Tell her! She's not moving that pikey into my room!' She sounds about twelve.

Luckily Mum shows some maturity. 'It's only temporary. She'll be out of here soon. It really won't affect you, Tamsyn.'

'She'd better not touch my stuff,' she says furiously.

If my sister's reaction was surprising, my best mate's was entirely predictable. I stop beside Mel in the college café, where she's lunching with Leah and Becky.

'I thought you might like to know that Suzie Grey is staying with me for the time being,' I inform her, my voice cold and clipped.

Mel's eyes open wide in surprise. 'Is that a good idea?'

'Um, yes actually. And it's all thanks to you.'

'Me?'

'Yes, you! If you hadn't been so nasty to her the other day I wouldn't have gone after her to see if she was all right. And then I would never have discovered just how truly awful her life is.'

'Really?' says Leah, sitting up straight.

'Why?' says Becky, her nose practically quivering with curiosity. 'What's happened to her?'

'I'm not at liberty to say,' I say frostily. 'But she deserves all the help she can get.'

'Yeah, right,' says Mel, sceptical as ever. 'Says who?'

'Says me.'

She rolls her eyes. 'She could be making it all up, you know. Have you thought of that?'

I feel anger sparking inside me, like tiny electric shocks. 'You have no idea what that girl's been through.'

'Yeah, give her a break, Mel,' says Leah.

'Poor thing,' echoes Becky, who agrees with everything Leah says. Mel starts to look uncomfortable.

'I'm just saying, be careful, that's all. You don't really know her. You know what you're like. There was this movie I saw once about a girl who moved in with another girl and she was evil—'

'I saw that!' squeals Becky, her eyes shining. 'It was brilliant. She took over . . .'

'Evil?' I repeat slowly. 'Are you saying Suzie Grey is evil?'

'No, I didn't say that,' says Mel, backtracking fast. 'I'm just saying—'

'I'll tell you what's evil, shall I?' I say self-righteously. 'Evil is when good men walk by and do nothing!'

I'd heard that saying somewhere, though I wasn't sure if I'd got it right. But it has the desired effect. Mel looks shamefaced.

'I didn't say she was evil. I didn't mean that. I just meant you don't know her. None of us do.'

'Well, get to know her then! You might have a pleasant surprise. She's no different from you or me, Mel. She just needs a break.'

'OK! OK! I get the picture! I'll try, just to shut you up.'

'So will I,' says Leah.

'And me,' chips in Becky.

'Thanks. Budge up, misery guts.' I plonk myself down next to Mel. She shakes her head at me.

'It's you I was thinking of, you know. You're too bloody soft for your own good.'

'That's funny, that's exactly what Suzie said about me. Maybe you two are going to get along after all.'

She grins. 'Yeah, right. If she changes into a vampire

123

after dark or her head spins around and she vomits green slime, don't blame me.'

'Be too late then. And it'll serve me right.' I flick the froth of her cappuccino at her and it catches her on the nose.

'Psycho!' she shrieks and does the same to me.

'Sicko!'

'Schizo!'

There's a full froth fight taking place between us with lots of squealing and giggling when, all of a sudden, Suzie appears at the table. Mel forces a smile on her face.

'Hey, Suzie,' she says. 'Wanna join us?'

16

On Saturday we are really busy at the salon. I haven't said much about my work at Herr Cutz, probably because there's so much else going on in my life, but I love my Saturday job. I've been there nearly a year now and because I'd spent all the summer holidays working there, I feel like a proper, full-time member of staff.

At least, usually I love it. But this particular Saturday morning it's totally manic. Shazza, the junior, has called in sick and Kay's out doing a wedding. Someone has managed to double-book a couple of clients for Gordon so Linda has to do some cuts while I take over her shampoo-and-sets. By midday, one woman has stomped out in a rage because she can't wait any longer, another's in a strop because Linda's cut her hair different from the way Kay does it, I've managed to drop a bottle of perming lotion on the floor and the whole place is stinking of ammonia, and Linda's threatening to walk.

'You need to take another Saturday girl on,' she points out, telling Gordon how to run the salon as usual, even though he's the one who owns it. 'My feet are killing me, I'm run ragged and there's no way any of us are going to get any lunch today.'

'I know,' mutters Gordon.

'It's only going to get worse over the run up to Christmas,' Linda persists.

'I'll advertise for one,' says Gordon through gritted teeth as he tries to mix a colour, extract payment from the cross client and answer the phone at the same time. 'But that's not going to help us now, is it? I can't magic someone up from nowhere.'

'I can!' I say, and they look at me as if I'm the fairy off the Christmas tree. 'There's a girl at college. She's only a first-year but she's very good. Her name's Suzie. I know she could do with the money . . .'

'Get her!' says Gordon, handing me the phone, and before I have time to wonder if this is a good idea, Suzie is installed in the salon.

She surprises us all. She picks things up so quickly, you'd swear she'd been there all her life. In a way Mel's right, Suzie is a perfect copycat. If she's told once she gets it and if she's not told she watches, sees what needs doing and does it. Before long she's welcoming clients in, offering them tea and coffee, chatting away to them while they're waiting so they don't notice how late we're running, making us coffee too, sweeping up without being asked, answering the phone and writing the appointments in the book.

At first I feel proud of her. Then, as Linda and Gordon keep nodding at each other and smiling, I start to feel a bit jealous, to be honest. *I'm* used to being the one who basks in their approval while Shazza gets in a muddle.

She's a quick learner, I have to say that for her. Plus she's smiley and friendly and outgoing too – not a bit like the morose little Suzie Grey she normally is – flitting happily around the salon like a busy little bird, making sure everything is clean and tidy and ready for us to do our jobs. And she nips out and buys us all sandwiches from the Co-op as well when she hears Linda complaining that her stomach thinks her throat's been cut.

Suzie Grey has found her niche in life.

At the end of the day, Gordon beams at her. 'Thanks sweetheart, you've been amazing. You've got yourself a Saturday job if you want it.'

Suzie's eyes light up. 'Are you serious?'

'Never been more serious in my life. See you next week, eight-thirty sharp.' He hands me my usual pay, five crisp ten-pound notes, and then gives her the same, to my surprise.

You've been here all day, she's *only been in for the afternoon. That's not fair*, says the mean little voice inside my head.

Gordon must have read my thoughts because he adds, 'You did us a big favour coming in like that, Suzie, I'm very grateful. Make sure you reimburse yourself for those sarnies from the till. And Indie, don't forget, those tips are to be divided up too.' He nods his head towards the jar standing on the reception desk and then looks at us both and laughs. 'You're like two peas in a pod, you two.'

Suzie grins at me. 'I'm going to like it here.' But I don't feel like smiling.

I share out the tips equally between us and try not to notice when she pulls out two tenners from the till for the sandwiches.

The Co-op must be more expensive than you thought.

''Bye, Lin! 'Bye, Gordon!' she trills as we make our exit.

You'd swear she'd been here for years.

Then I feel ashamed. I know what's making me moody. It's not just the money. It's the fact that she's waltzed in and taken over and made a success of it. On my patch!

Get over yourself, Indie, I tell myself sternly. You invited her! Be glad for her. She was made up with the money she'd earned, you could tell.

No wonder, says the mean little voice. *She must have got eighty or ninety quid in her pocket, what with her pay and the tips and the money she's taken for the sarnies.*

On the way home, Suzie yaps away nonstop about the salon but I can't shake off my black mood. She's like a dog on a lead that's got itself entangled in my life. I can't move without her tripping me up. Then suddenly she says, 'Hang on a minute!' and disappears inside a shop. I wait for her sourly by the entrance. Two minutes later she comes out and thrusts a bag into my hands.

'What's this?'

'Present for you,' she says.

'What for?'

'To say thank you. For getting me the job. For taking me in. For everything.'

I pull a top out of the bag. She looks at me anxiously.

'That's the one, isn't it? The one you've been fancying for ages? If you don't like it, you can take it back and choose something else. Look, I've got the receipt.'

And now I feel really, really mean. She gets some

money at last and what's the first thing she does with it? Spends it on me.

'It's fabulous,' I say and give her a hug. What is the matter with me? I am such a fraud. Everyone thinks I'm really kind taking Suzie on board, but I'm not. Look at me. I've got myself in a right mood, just because she's done well at the salon and Gordon likes her and has given her a job. Some friend I am. I should be pleased for her.

I am pleased for her! Inside, I give myself a good shake. She's on her way now. Soon she'll be able to cope on her own and be out of my hair (ha ha!) for good.

And it turns out, I'm right. Over the next couple of weeks, Suzie blossoms. I'm sure it's the salon that's done it. In no time at all she's washing hair and doing a bit of blow-drying and most of the stuff that I do in the salon. Except for cutting. Gordon won't let her do that. Yet.

It does wonders for her confidence. Gradually, she settles down, both at home and college. Tamsyn, having checked out her old room periodically and found it practically untouched, stops stressing about her. Mum and Dad refuse to take the money she earns at the salon for rent when Suzie offers it to them. 'Any friend of

130

Indigo's is a friend of ours,' Dad says, though I'm not absolutely sure this applies to Rick. Even Mel, who's railed against Suzie from the start, makes an effort.

As Suzie is accepted by everyone at home, work and college, the strange, withdrawn loner turns into a version of everyone else.

Or to be strictly honest, another version of me.

'So, let me see if I've got this right.'

Mrs Moffat's voice, out of the blue, startles me.

'By now Suzie was living with you, going to college with you, working with you and hanging out with your friends.'

'Yeah, so what?' Immediately I'm on the defensive. Put like that, it was surprising how quickly Suzie had infiltrated my life.

'That's quite a commitment.'

'That's what Rick said. Actually, he said a lot more than that.'

'Rick still didn't like her.'

'He was the one person who couldn't stand her. Especially when Scarlett came.'

'Maybe you'd like to tell me about it. But first of all, can you clarify something else for me.'

'What?'

'Who, exactly, is Scarlett?'

I laugh. A short, bitter bark of a laugh.

'Scarlett is Suzie.'

17

Suzie Grey was . . . grey.

Scarlett was brilliant red, tinged with orange.

Suzie was a quiet little mouse, scurrying round the cracks and corners of other people's lives.

Scarlett was a dominant brightly-coloured macaw, slap-bang in the middle of things, marking out her territory with loud squawks.

Suzie was sad, timid, apologetic, isolated and vulnerable.

Scarlett was happy, confident, defiant, popular and powerful.

Suzie left.

And Scarlett arrived.

But it didn't happen overnight. It took place over a period of weeks. Months even.

Looking back, it was the haircut that started it all off.

Then the makeover.

Then the clothes.

Then the hair colour.

Then the job. Definitely the job.

The day Scarlett finally took over was on our anniversary. Mine and Rick's. The anniversary of our first date. It was a Sunday. Rick and I had planned to spend it together. I'd bought him a boy-racer keyring, for a laugh and also as a way of saying, you'll be driving again soon. The weather forecast was good and we were going to go for an autumnal picnic together. His idea. 'That is so romantic!' Leah had sighed. I had to admit, I was looking forward to it.

I was in Suzie's bedroom at the front of the house, borrowing back a sweater.

No wonder Tamsyn had stopped worrying about the cuckoo in her nest. Suzie had not put a mark on her room.

'It looks better on you,' she says as I pull it on.

'It looks exactly the same as it does on you.'

'Nah, it suits your colouring better. Your skin-tone is darker than mine.'

'Style guru! What are you like?' Whatever happened to that drab little mouse who first arrived on the scene not so long ago? 'You have totally reinvented yourself, you know.'

'I have, haven't I?' She looks pleased. 'New look, new friends, new job, new place to live. And it's all thanks to you.'

I try to look modest but I can't help grinning. That's probably the closest Suzie Grey has ever got to gratitude.

Then she adds, 'Now all I need is a new name,' and I nearly choke.

'Are you serious?'

'Yeah. Yeah, I think I am. It makes sense, doesn't it?' Her eyes light up. 'I'll be safe then, won't I? He'll never be able to trace me, not with a new name. What d'you think?'

'I don't know. I don't know how easy it is to change your name, just like that . . .'

'It's simple. If it's your Christian name you just call yourself anything you want.' Bizarrely I wonder if she's done this before. Her face is bright. 'Help me choose one, Ind.'

'Um, I don't know, what's your favourite?'

She shrugs.

'Mine's Jessica,' I say helpfully. She pulls a face.

'Start at the beginning of the alphabet, then. Abby, Annie, Angela . . .'

'Bor-ing. Something different.'

I look around for inspiration. Outside, brittle-brown leaves are falling from the old sycamore tree. 'Autumn?

Summer?' I suggest. 'Or maybe a month. Not October. How about April? May? June? Those are all real names.'

'No,' she groans. 'I want something different. Like your name!'

'My name's a colour. What about Violet or Rose?'

'Too soft and sweet. I'm not soft or sweet, am I?'

No, definitely not. And she wasn't grey any more either. I've never seen her so animated.

'What would I be if I was a colour?' she keeps on. 'Something that would suit the new me.'

Today she is fiery, burning with energy. If she was a colour she would be . . .

'Red!' I say wildly. 'Ruby! Or Cherry! Or Scarlet!'

'Scarlet!' She pounces on the name like a cat on a bird. 'I love it! Scarlet's who I want to be. Scarlett – with a double T. Oh, I've made up a rhyme.'

As the doorbell rings downstairs she dances round the room with her arms in the air, chanting,

'Scarlett's who I want to be.

Scarlett with a double T!'

She looks so pleased with herself, so giddy, like someone half her age, I have to laugh.

'Scarlett Grey? Isn't that a bit weird?'

'It'll do for the time being.' But then she comes to a halt by the window and says, 'Uh-oh!'

138

I go across and spot it at once.

A Triumph Herald is standing by the kerb.

Taking the stairs three at a time I fling the front door open wide before Rick has even had a chance to ring the bell. He laughs in surprise.

'What do you think you're doing?' My voice raps out like a machine-gun, hitting the target full-on. His smile fades.

'Going for a picnic – aren't we?'

'Not in that, we're not!'

'But . . . I thought we'd head for the coast. It's a beautiful day.'

'Rick! You're banned!'

'Indie, chill out! Nothing's going to happen.' He tries to put his arms round me but I step back.

'You could get into really serious trouble,' I remind him, but he shakes his head, laughing at me.

'Come on, Indie, it's a special day. I'm not going to get stopped. I'll drive it like a hearse.'

'Someone could see you. You could be reported.'

'Nobody knows!'

He was right. For some reason he hadn't got into the court round-up in the weekly paper. We could probably get away with it, barring accidents. I am *so* tempted.

'The sun is shining, the roof is down, the champagne's

on ice!' he wheedles, sensing me weakening, and I find myself laughing back at him.

I dangle the keyring in front of him. 'This is for you,' I say and he takes it from me and kisses me on the lips. Then he whispers in my ear.

'Remember that night in the summer? We could always take our clothes off and go for a dip . . .' And though I giggle because I know he's joking, my insides turn to slush and I know he's won. I'd go to the ends of the earth with Rick if he wanted me to.

But then I sense him drawing away. Suzie has appeared behind us. He is really not happy with the fact that she's kipping down at mine.

'Take care,' Suzie says quietly and I sense the warning in her voice and come to my senses. She knew Rick was banned from driving. I'd told her. Maybe Rick had told some of his mates too.

This is madness.

'I'm not going in the car!' I say emphatically and Rick groans.

'Indie! I've been planning this for ages. It's a special occasion.'

My voice softens. 'We could go to the park. We can walk there.'

'I don't want to go to the park.' His voice is as sulky

and disappointed as a six-year-old's.

'Ahh, diddums!' comes Suzie's voice from behind me. Quiet, but it carries.

'What did you say?' Rick's voice is equally quiet. And chilling.

'Catch a bus,' says Suzie.

'Excuse me?'

'You don't have to use your car,' she points out. 'You can get a bus somewhere. For your little *pic-nic*.'

She emphasizes the word tauntingly, making it sound childish instead of a wonderful, romantic thing to do. Rick's eyes blaze.

'Remind me. What has this got to do with you?'

'Ri-ick!' I protest, but he looks at her with undisguised dislike.

'Well, it was all right till she started poking her nose in.'

'*She's* got a name. It's Scarlett to you,' she informs him icily.

'Scarlett!' Rick's jaw drops open. 'Since when?'

'Since now.'

His lip curls into an unattractive sneer. 'What sort of poncey name is that?'

'Um, one like your girlfriend's? Indigo. Scarlet. They're colours, didn't you know?'

'You are one weird bitch! And you're a fake, d'you know that?'

'Rick! Stop being so rude.'

'She is! Can't you see what she's doing? She's copying you again. She's taking you over!'

'Fine!' yells Suzie. 'Do what you want! Drive without a licence, you tosser! What do I care?'

Rick's face darkens. He turns to me. 'You told her!'

'I didn't mean to!'

He loses it then, swearing at us both. I try to calm him down but he's in melt-down – I've never seen him like this before in my life. He says I care more about her than him and soon I've had enough and slam the door in his face. He hammers on it, calling my name, kicking it in frustration, and Mum appears from the kitchen, looking worried. Next thing I hear is the engine revving and the car tearing away, tyres screaming.

I lean back against the inside of the door, trembling from head to foot.

'What on earth is going on?' asks Mum.

I shake my head, trying to get rid of that picture of Rick, eyes mad, spitting with rage, out of control.

'Lovers' tiff,' explains Suzie, taking charge, her voice calm now. 'It'll blow over. It's nothing.'

18

When I've calmed down, Suzie and I end up going to town.

I mean *Scarlett* and I. She insists on being called Scarlett now.

'Come on!' she says, grabbing a large shopping bag and slinging it over her shoulder. 'Let's hit the shops. Thanks to you, I've got money to spend for once in my life.'

Bring back Suzie, I think grimly. She never used to be this bossy. Or happy. It's weird, it seems like the more difficult my life becomes, hers correspondingly becomes more blissful. It's not fair!

Even though I've been promising myself some new clothes, I don't feel like shopping. I'm meant to be celebrating my first anniversary with my boyfriend. But the alternative is being interrogated by my mother as to why Rick and I have had a row, and I can hardly explain it's because he's driving around when he's banned. Not that she wouldn't take my side. But I don't want to give her and Dad any more ammunition against him. So I slap on some make-up and do as I'm told.

It's Sunday but the high street is busy. Scarlett's been saving up her wages from the salon and is on a mission to kit herself out in new season trends. For a late-starter she's making up for a lot of lost ground.

We go into a big department store and head for the designer floor. Scarlett grabs handfuls of clothes from the various outlets and makes straight for the changing rooms. She's got far too many, more than she's allowed to take in, so she leaves some on the rail inside the room and disappears into a cubicle. I follow her into the one next door, carrying a short leather jacket just to show willing and a pair of trousers, though my heart's not in it.

Scarlett, though, is having a ball. She keeps dashing into my cubicle to show me what she looks like. I have to admit, she looks good in everything. Her hair really suits her and she's thin as a rake. She's like a walking coat-hanger.

The trousers look rubbish on me.

'Why aren't you trying things on?' she asks, reappearing

with yet more items. The assistant's given up trying to keep count and is just letting her get on with it. She pours herself into a pair of skin-tight jeans and turns sideways to admire her reflection in the mirror.

'I'm not in the mood.'

''Course you are.' She wriggles her way back out of the jeans and hands them to me. 'Here, try these on with that jacket.'

Once again I find myself obeying the new assertive Scarlett as she continues to throw outfits on and off. Reluctantly I squeeze myself into the jeans and zip them up and Scarlett squeals with delight.

'They look fantastic!'

She's right, they do. I slip the soft black jacket on. It is totally seductive, the look, the touch, the smell of it. I thrust my hands into the pockets and study my reflection in the mirror, unsmiling, my head to one side.

'You look a-ma-zing!' says Scarlett, and at last a smile finds its way to my lips. 'You have got to buy that!'

I know. Suddenly I want this outfit, these jeans, this coat, more than anything I've ever wanted before in my life. Especially the coat. At last I understand how Rick feels about cars. I've fallen in love with a leather jacket.

I look at the price tag. And groan.

It is way, way out of my league.

'Buy it,' repeats Scarlett.

'I can't! It's too expensive.'

'How much?'

'Too much.'

'So? You can afford it.'

I laugh derisively.

'Have you got enough money in your account?' she persists.

I hesitate, staring at myself in the mirror. I totally, utterly love this jacket. 'I have, actually . . .' I say slowly, 'but I can't spend this much on a coat. I need it for other things.'

'Like what?' Her voice is soft, taunting. 'Paying your boyfriend's latest fine?'

'NO!' Her words sting me to the core. She must think I'm his pathetic lapdog. 'He hasn't asked me to, if that's what you're thinking!'

'I didn't say he had. I just know what you're like.' She grins at me and I can't lie to her.

'If he can't find the money, I may offer to help. So what?'

'Indie, stop it! So long as Rick knows you'll bail him out, he'll keep on doing stupid stuff. Make him stand on his own two feet for once. Believe me, I know what I'm talking about!'

I know she does, she's been there. I mean, Rick's nothing like her ex, he's a nice guy, but he does have a tendency to land himself in hot water and I do have a tendency to come to his rescue. Every time. It's me – I'm the problem, not him. I make myself responsible for his actions.

I stare at myself in the mirror again. I turn to the left, then to the right. I practically twist my head off checking my back view. I gaze at myself straight-on, doing my special posing pouty-face, the one I keep for trying things on. It looks good from every angle.

'You look beautiful,' says Scarlett.

'Ohhhh,' I moan to myself in an agony of indecision, 'I don't know what to do.'

'OK, so what's the problem?'

'Duh! The price? It's mega-expensive.'

'Well, there's ways around that.'

'Such as?'

She leans towards me and her voice drops to a whisper. 'Nick it.'

Time stops in that cubicle in that store on that Sunday in the high street.

Then Scarlett grins and time moves on again. 'Only joking! You should see your face!'

'I know that!' But she's shaken me. I feel light-headed,

giddy, out of control. There's only one way to put that right. I place the coat back on its hanger and hear myself saying, 'Come on. I'm buying it.'

'Yaaaay!' she says. Then, 'I'll just finish up here, see what I want. I'll be with you in a sec.'

I go outside and walk up to the counter before I can change my mind. I have never spent this much on myself or anyone else for that matter in my life – except for things for my course, which don't count. The assistant sighs as she takes the coat from me.

'It's gorgeous.' She smiles longingly, stroking its soft texture, and I feel stirrings of pride that soon it will be mine.

'Place your card in the machine,' she says. Then, 'Enter your PIN number.'

I tap in my number and breathe a long sigh of gratification. Too late to turn back. The coat belongs to me now. My gift to myself. My guilty pleasure.

Beside me Scarlett appears with a pile of clothes over her arms. Her jaw drops and she gasps as she spots the price on the machine. Three hundred pounds.

'Told you you should've nicked it,' she says and the assistant's eyes automatically move up to hers. 'Joke!' she adds sharply and dumps the garments unceremoniously on the counter. The girl ignores her and completes my transaction but I notice her smile has vanished now and is replaced by tight-lipped disapproval as she folds the jacket carefully into a large store bag.

My joy evaporates. What have I done? I can't afford this. What on earth came over me?

Scarlett came over me. It's all her fault.

I sound like a little kid caught out at school. *It was her, Miss! She made me do it!*

What on earth is wrong with me? I've got a mind of my own!

I wander away from the till as Scarlett pays for her purchases with a wad of notes, clutching my store bag. All pleasure in my new jacket is gone. I don't want it any more, but that assistant will definitely think I'm up to something if I ask for my money back. My chest tightens and I feel cold, panicky, not a bit like me. Then my phone bleeps and I welcome the distraction as a text comes through.

I'M SORRY!

Rick. I knew he would be, once he'd calmed down. There is absolutely no malice in Rick; he's just a risk-taker with a very short fuse. Plus he spends far too much on cars. I look wryly at the bag in my hand and sigh. Who am I to talk? Strangely, his text makes me feel more centred. Let's face it, we all do stupid things, even me.

I wish I'd just jumped in the car with him and gone for a picnic.

Scarlett appears beside me, laden down with bags, looking pleased with herself. But her face changes as she sees me on my phone.

'Rick?'

'Who else?'

'Who else indeed?'

Something about her voice makes me take note. She really doesn't like him, does she? Well that's her problem, not mine. 'I'm going home,' I say and text him back to let him know I'm on my way. Scarlett stamps along beside me, stiff and silent with disapproval, but I don't care. This is my life, Scarlett, not yours.

Rick is sitting outside my house, waiting for me, a wicker hamper by his feet. Scarlett disappears indoors as I walk up to him.

'I've just seen your parents going out,' he says conversationally.

'What have you done with the car?' I ask.

'It's back in the garage,' he says sheepishly. 'Where it belongs.'

'Good,' I say. 'Best place for it. Come on, you – upstairs. We need to talk.'

We barely make it through my bedroom door before his arms are around me and he's raining me with apologies. *He's sorry, he's an idiot, he doesn't know what he was thinking of, he just wanted to go back to the beach where we'd had such a good time, he wanted to make today really special for me, he'd planned it for ages, this had been the best year of his life since he met me, he loves me so much, he doesn't deserve someone like me, I'm the best thing that ever happened to him, he doesn't know what he'd do without me, I keep him on the straight and narrow, he'd never felt like this about anyone before . . .*

I stop him with a kiss. And then, safe in the knowledge that my parents are not around, we make up.

19

Afterwards we end up having our anniversary picnic in bed, eating Thai roast chicken with mango and apple salad, and individual strawberry and almond tarts, washed down with champagne. Rick bought it all from the posh new deli on the high street. He is so sweet. No wonder he was cross with me, he'd been planning it for ages. I'm wearing my new leather jacket and not much else. Rick loves it, by the way.

'You look really sexy in that,' he says, pouring me another glass of vintage champagne and popping a rich chocolate truffle into my mouth. Expense is no object with my boyfriend.

'Sexy, not dirty?' I say anxiously.

'Well, maybe just a bit dirty at this precise moment,' he grins and reaches for me again.

I love him so much. Now I'm safe again in his arms, I love my jacket too, though I'm not going to tell him how much it cost, not after all my nagging at him to be careful with money. But after a couple more glasses of bubbly, I find myself confessing to him anyway. He thinks it's funny.

'Indigo Moore, letting her hair down at last! About time too.'

Rick's so non-judgemental.

Not like me.

If he'd spent that much on a jacket I'd have given him hell.

But then, Rick doesn't worry about money.

Not like me.

'Have you paid your fine yet?' I ask, gazing up at his face.

'Yeah.'

'All of it?' I say in surprise.

'Yeah, all of it.'

'How come? How could you afford to? What about all this . . . ?' I indicate the remains of the picnic, the empty bottle of champagne, and his mood changes.

'It's sorted, Indie.'

He rolls off me, on to his back, and stares up at the ceiling, his hands behind his head. I've upset him, harping on like that about the fine. I prop myself up on my elbow to study him. The laughter lines round his beautiful eyes have disappeared to be replaced by a frown between his eyebrows. I've done that to him. 'I'm sorry,' I say softly and stroke his cheek. He turns his head to me.

'Don't you trust me?' he asks and in answer, I lower my lips to his.

Then the door bursts open and we burst apart.

'TA-DAH!' Scarlett is posing in the doorway in a brand new skimpy top and tight jeans, bottom stuck out, concave belly on display. Her hair is gelled to a shine and her white face is made up like a vamp, with thick black eyeliner flicked up at the corners and bright red lips. She's buckled a belt round her neck like a dog-collar. One hand is on her hip, the other held high in the air, brandishing something.

Now she really does look dirty.

'What the hell?' Rick swears loudly and dives for cover under the sheet. If it wasn't so awful, it would be farcical. Though I can't help feeling relieved it's her, not my dad, who's caught us in bed together.

'Oops, sorry!' she says. 'Wasn't expecting you to be – you know . . .'

'Obviously,' I say, not knowing whether to laugh or cry. Considering she's just walked in on two people

155

during a pretty intimate moment she doesn't look embarrassed. Not half as embarrassed as we are. She doesn't even barge straight back out again, which is what I would do. She just looks at us and laughs.

'I just wanted to show you my new gear and give you these,' she says and chucks me what's in her hand. I reach out automatically to catch it. It's the jeans I tried on in the shop. 'Little present from me to you, to go with your new jacket. Looks nice, by the way.'

She turns to go and then looks back at us with a grin. 'Sorry,' she repeats, though she doesn't seem the least bit remorseful. 'I didn't mean to interrupt. You can carry on now.'

'What the hell!' snarls Rick, emerging from beneath the sheet as she shuts the door behind her.

'Nice of her though,' I say, inspecting the jeans. 'She knew I liked them. They cost loads.'

'She probably nicked them,' he says savagely. 'She takes exactly what she wants, that one.'

Poor Rick. He should know. She's just taken his dignity and left it in tatters. She probably did it on purpose.

Either that or she was trying to impress him.

The next day I wear my new leather jacket to college and everybody loves it.

'You can tell quality,' says Leah, stroking it admiringly.

'Money-bags!' groans Mel. 'It's not fair. I'm skint.'

'You should have worked through the summer like me instead of blowing it all on a holiday in Ibiza!' I say smugly. 'Payback time.'

'Your jeans are nice too,' she remarks.

'Scarlett bought these for me.'

'Who's Scarlett?'

'I am.' Scarlett puts her arm round my shoulders. She's dressed in new clothes too and is looking really cool. 'I've changed my name,' she explains unnecessarily. 'I'm not Suzie any more.'

Mel's jaw drops open. 'Why Scarlett?'

'Two shades on the colour spectrum. Scarlett and Indigo.'

Mel stares at her like she's gone mad. 'You two are like bloody peas in a pod,' she mutters. Then she adds, 'I thought you were broke?'

'I am now,' says Scarlett. 'I'm spent out. But on Saturday I'll be in-pocket again because I'll be working at the salon. Anyway, I wanted to say thank you to Indie for being so good to me – putting me up, finding me a job. I owe her a lot.'

'Yeah,' says Mel. 'That's pretty obvious.' Her voice is flat with an edge of sarcasm but Scarlett doesn't appear to notice. She looks around shyly at everyone.

'I owe you all,' she says. 'For accepting me, letting me be your friend. I don't know how much Indie's told you, but it's not been easy for me, moving here on my own. But you've all been great. I don't know how I can ever repay you.'

'Aahh!' Leah and Becky and the other girls go all dewy-eyed and move in on Scarlett for a group hug. Only Mel hangs back.

'Nice speech,' she says under her breath. Then, knowing I heard what she said, she shrugs. 'Just call me cynical!'

I feel a wave of irritation. Poor Scarlett, she just can't win. Look how far she has come since those first sad days at college. She is doing her best to create a new life for herself but no matter how hard she tries, for some people it would never be enough. Like my moody boyfriend and my sarky best mate, for instance.

They're just jealous of how important she's become to me.

Mel must've realized she's overstepped the mark because she changes the subject. 'Are you and Rick going to the Christmas Ball this year?'

'Yeah, guess so.'

'Only, the tickets are going on sale today.'

'It's not even November!'

'I know, but there's a limit on numbers and they go straight away. I'm buying mine at lunchtime. I expect Rick will be getting yours.'

I sigh, remembering that he'd just forked out for his massive fine. The ball was a brilliant night out but it didn't come cheap. 'Doubt it. He's a bit strapped for cash at the moment. I'd better get some money out.'

'Me too.'

We stroll over to the cash machine together and Mel goes first. Then it's my turn. But to my surprise, a notice flashes up to say there are insufficient funds in my account.

'What?'

'Oops!' says Mel, peering close to read the words on the screen. 'Looks like you've been spending more than you thought, Indie love. I knew that jacket must've cost a bit.'

'But – there should still be money in it, plus there's an overdraft facility . . .' I take the card out and try it again, requesting a lesser amount. The same message appears. I groan with frustration.

'I just don't get it. There must be some mistake. It's this stupid cashpoint!'

'It's not like you,' concedes Mel. 'You're the careful

one. Look, I'll take some more out so you can get your tickets.'

'No, I can't let you do that, you said you're skint . . .' But it's too late and once again the machine does as she bids and spews banknotes out obediently. She hands them straight to me, waving away my protests.

'It's all right. Pay me back once you've sorted it out. You don't want to miss the ball. Hottest couple last year, remember?'

'Thanks, Mel. I'm sure it's a mistake. I'll pop into the bank this afternoon and sort it.'

But I can't help feeling worried. This has never happened before. Mel stares at me, concern in her eyes. We've always been able to read each other like a book. She looks like she wants to say something but doesn't know how to broach the subject.

'What?'

'No one else could have had access to your account, could they?'

'Like who?'

She hesitates but then turns around, her eyes sweeping the common room. They come to rest on Scarlett in her new gear, chatting and laughing with the group of girls we've just left. Mel bites her lip.

'Oh, come on!' I protest. But despite myself an image

of Scarlett standing at the department store till yesterday with a big wad of notes in her hand leaps into my mind.

'I'm not accusing anyone!' says Mel quietly. 'But look at her! You've got to admit, she's been flashing the cash around lately.'

20

When I get home that night I'm seriously pissed off. Things are worse than I thought. At the bank I'd discovered not only was my account empty, I'm overdrawn as well. Like Mel said, it's not like me to be so careless.

As I pass Tam's old room I see Scarlett through the open door. She's posing in front of the mirror in yet another new outfit and her bed is heaped with clothes. When she sees my reflection she twirls around and says, 'Hi!' and I hesitate but then I carry straight on upstairs to my room. I need to go online and check my statements.

When I've tapped into my account I can see immediately that I was right, I shouldn't have bought that jacket. I'd gone right up to the limit of my overdraft to pay for it without realizing. I'd have to take it back.

But it was too late for that. I'd already worn it.

How did this happen? When I paid for that jacket I thought I had at least five hundred pounds in my account, plus overdraft facilities.

As I move down my statement, noting the list of outgoings, my stomach plummets. What was wrong with me? It looked like I'd been taking out way more cash than I'd realized. Yes, I'd been making far too much use of the cashpoint at college. Now I was broke and it served me right. No, it was worse than that, I was in debt. I had a huge overdraft to pay off.

I look more closely. Hang on a minute. There's a big withdrawal here for two hundred pounds. I never took that much money out in one go. What day was that on?

Last Friday. And here, the day before, was another one for one hundred pounds. What the hell was going on?

Shit! My mouth goes dry. Mel was right. Someone has been tapping into my account.

There's a knock on the door. I turn round so fast I frighten the life out of Scarlett.

'What's up?' she says. 'You made me jump!' She's smiling but her eyes are wary. 'What are you doing?' she asks, her eyes fixed on the screen.

'Checking my bank account,' I say flatly.

'Uh-oh!' she says, like she's expecting me to laugh but I don't respond. 'Everything OK?' she asks.

'Why? Shouldn't it be?'

I glare at her and she laughs nervously. 'Well, you must have made a pretty big hole in it buying that jacket.'

'You can't make a hole in nothing.'

'What d'you mean?'

I don't answer. After a while she says, 'Indie? What is going on?'

'You tell me.'

She frowns. 'Stop freaking me out. Why are you acting like this?'

'Like what?'

'Like I've done something to upset you.'

'Have you?'

'I don't know!' she says wildly. 'Tell me what's wrong and I'll tell you if I've done it!'

I take a deep breath. 'Someone's been taking money from my account.'

'You're joking! Who?'

'I don't know.'

She comes close up to peer at the screen and immediately I shut it down. She looks at me, confused, then backs away like I've attacked her. 'Oh no!' she gasps. 'You think it's me, don't you?'

'I don't know what to think! All I know is someone's emptied me out.'

'You think I'd steal from you?' Her face is stricken.

'Well, somebody has!'

'So it's me? I'm the prime suspect?'

'I didn't say that. But—'

'But what?'

'Well, you are a bit flush at the moment, you've got to admit. All that money you were flashing round yesterday . . . all those clothes on your bed . . . the jeans you bought me . . .'

My words, which have left my mouth at a breakneck speed, slow down to a grinding halt as her face hardens. 'Don't forget the top I bought you too,' she reminds me.

'Yeah,' I say awkwardly. 'That as well.'

'Bitch!' The word makes my ears ring like a slap on the cheek. 'They were presents. From me to you. To say thank you.'

'I know! I know!' I say wildly.

'I paid for those out of my own money!'

'I know you did!'

Her lip curls into a horrible sneer. 'You think I'm a thief don't you?'

'No! I don't!'

'Liar!' She pushes her face up so close to mine that I find myself backing away from her warm breath, the moisture that springs from her mouth to land on my lip, on my cheek, as she spits out her venom at me. 'I feel like slapping you! You make out you're so nice, so kind, but you're just the same as everyone else!'

'I'm sorry—'

'It's too late for that, you cow! Anyway, I can tell you're just saying it, I know you don't believe me. But I can prove I never took your stinking, rotten money!'

'You don't have to do that!'

'Yes I do!' she says, cursing loudly at me as she storms out of the room and down the stairs. I'm trembling all over. Two minutes later, she's back again with a receipt which she thrusts into my hands.

'Read it!' she says. I run my eyes down the bit of paper. My jeans are there plus a few other items, a top, leggings, a skirt, a cardigan. I struggle to keep my voice steady.

'Look,' I say. 'I don't think you pinched my money. But this receipt doesn't prove a thing. It proves you bought my jeans but it doesn't prove how you got the money to pay for them. You bought loads more stuff than this yesterday, I've seen all those clothes on your bed. How could you afford them all?'

'Duh! That's the point, stupid. I couldn't.'

'What?'

She looks at me pityingly, like I've got a screw loose or something. 'I nicked them! Obviously.'

I stare at her, bewildered. 'When?'

'When you were having a nice little chat with that snooty assistant. I was busy snipping off security tags, putting that lot on under my clothes. Look!' My head jerks back as she brandishes a sharp tool like a screwdriver in my face. 'You want to get one of these, they come in handy!' She sneers at my look of alarm. 'Naah, on second thoughts, you'd get the security ink everywhere.'

'You were shoplifting!' I gaze at her horrified. 'She must've thought I was in on it as well!'

'Doubt it. You're an innocent, anyone can tell that!' The way she says it makes me feel inadequate rather than honest and upright.

I try to get my head around what she's just told me. 'So, you admit it. You did steal from that shop. So why are you mad at me?'

'You don't get it, do you?' She stares at me with round, sad eyes, all anger gone, like I've let her down.

'No, I don't. Tell me.'

'Because I never stole from *you*! I wouldn't do that! You're my friend – or I thought you were. I bought those jeans for you, fair and square, out of my earnings from the salon, because I wanted to say thank you for all you've done for me. I never nicked them, I just took stuff for myself. And you know something? I would never, ever, not in a million years, hack into your bloody account.'

Her eyes are wide with outraged virtue and her disappointment in me is palpable, like I can reach out and touch the barrier I've somehow managed to erect between us.

'But – it's still wrong to shoplift!' I protest feebly. 'Stealing from shops is just as wrong as stealing from someone you know . . .'

'No it's not!' she says sternly. 'Don't be daft.' Once again I get the feeling that as far as she's concerned, my values are highly questionable. 'Those big stores rip us off all the time, tempting us to spend money on things we can't afford. It's not right! That's why the whole country is in debt.'

I almost feel like laughing. She's so self-righteous, she sounds just like my dad.

'But,' she says fiercely, staring me straight in the eye, 'I would NEVER, EVER, nick from a mate.'

Honour among thieves. That's what they call it. I should've understood this, I've watched enough TV dramas.

'I'm sorrrreeeee!' I groan. After a while she relents.

'So you should be!' she grumbles, then she waves the tag-remover at me. 'I'll show you how to use this if you like.'

'No, it's all right,' I say hastily, 'I'm fine thanks.' Then I sit down heavily on my bed and groan. 'But the fact remains, Scarlett, someone has been helping themselves to money from my account and I haven't a clue who it is.'

She's silent. So silent it makes me look up.

'To anyone but you it would be bleeding obvious,' she says and pity is written all over her face.

21

'What? What d'you mean?' I ask, even though there's no need. I know exactly what – or who – she's getting at.

'Work it out, Indie. Who could've had access to your account?'

'Nobody I know of.'

'Family? Friends?'

I frown. 'Don't be daft. They wouldn't take money out of my account. Anyway, nobody's got my details.'

'Nobody?'

'No!' But my denial is too quick. Rick had my details. Only last week, tied up with work, I'd passed him my card and asked him to order some course books for me over the internet. She was there at the time.

'Poor Rick.' Scarlett's tone is soft, insidious. 'He's in a right mess. He owes you money, he owes money on the car and now he's got a five-hundred-pound fine to pay on top. How much did you say was missing from your account?'

'I didn't,' I say crisply. 'And that's where you're wrong. He's already paid his fine.'

'Has he?' Her eyes widen in surprise and I feel a fleeting surge of satisfaction which immediately ebbs as she says, 'Well, there you are then!'

'What the hell are you suggesting?' I glare at her, outraged. 'Rick would never steal from me!'

'Not steal, no. Of course he wouldn't,' she says evenly. 'But maybe he borrowed it, without you knowing, just to pay off his fine.'

'Why would he do that? He knows I'd give it to him if he asked.'

'He's not going to do that, is he?' She looks at me as if I don't understand the first thing about men. Maybe I don't. 'He's a proud guy, Rick. No, I reckon he borrowed it, just till pay day. Then he would've replaced it and you'd have been none the wiser.'

'I would've seen it on the statement,' I say sulkily.

'Yeah, eventually, maybe. But by that time the money would've been safely back in your account. And even if you had worked out it was Rick who had . . . *borrowed* it, he'd have apologized and turned on the charm and everything in the garden would've been rosy again. You know what he's like. He can twist you right round his little finger!'

I stare at her sadly. Funny that. That's what Mel said about her, more or less. I must be a real loser if I'm that easily exploited. But the awful thing is, I think she may be right.

And then my phone rings. I answer it and tell Rick I'll see him at mine in half an hour.

He arrives looking pleased with himself, clutching two tickets for the Christmas Ball. I take mine out of the top drawer and say, 'Snap!' and his face falls. Then he says, 'Take yours back.'

'No, you take yours back,' I say automatically.

'No, you take yours back,' he insists and puts his arms round me. But I stand there stiff and unresponsive as he tries to kiss me and he stares down at me, puzzled.

'What's up?'

'Actually, I do need to take my tickets back. I can't afford them any more.'

'OK. Sorted. No problem.'

'But you can't afford them either.'

'Indie, stop worrying. I'm not that broke that I can't take my beautiful girl to the Ball.'

He's laughing at me. I love him when he laughs. That's what I fell for in the first place, his smile, his easy manner . . .

He'd have turned on the charm and everything in the garden would be rosy again.

'How come?' I say, my voice suddenly harsh. 'You must be. You paid your fine.'

'What is this?' The smile disappears and a small frown appears between his brows, like he doesn't understand what's going on.

'You did pay your fine, didn't you?'

His tongue clicks impatiently. 'I told you I did . . .'

'But how could you?'

'How could I what?'

'Pay your fine.'

'Indie? What are you getting at?'

'Where did you get the money from?'

'Never you mind. It's nothing to do with you.'

'Rick, I need to know . . .'

'What are you going over old ground for?'

'Rick—'

'Indie, stop keeping on . . .'

'Rick, did you take money out of my account?'

He recoils as if suddenly I've been afflicted by some horrible, contagious disease.

'What did you say?'

'There's money missing from my account.'

'How much?'

'A lot. Hundreds.'

'And you think I stole it?'

'No! I thought you might have . . . *borrowed* it, to pay your fine?'

He is staring at me, stunned, and my heart stands still. His face says it all. Rick can never hide his feelings.

I have made a dreadful, dreadful mistake.

'I'm sorry,' I say and put my hand out towards him, but he steps back.

'You think I'd do that to you?' he asks, bewildered.

'No! I was just asking . . .'

He shakes his head, once, twice, like he's trying to dispel what I said. 'I can't believe you'd think I'd steal from you,' he repeats and it cuts me to the quick.

'I didn't mean it!'

'I wouldn't steal from anyone, let alone you,' he says and I know it's true.

Behind him, Scarlett appears in the doorway. 'Everything all right?' she asks and Rick spins around.

'You!' His face is furious as he turns back to me. 'Did she put you up to this?'

'Up to what?' asks Scarlett, and you'd swear she didn't

175

have a clue what he was talking about.

'Don't play the innocent with me! You told Indie I'd stolen her money!' he says ferociously and her expression changes.

'Well, you did, didn't you?' she asks.

'Bitch!' He's struggling desperately to keep control but she's smirking, goading him on, and for one awful second I'm scared that Rick, my sweet, kind, easy-going boy who to my knowledge has never raised his hand in temper to a soul, is going to hit her.

She's going too far. What's she playing at?

'Rick,' I wail, 'it doesn't matter what *she* thinks! *I* believe you!'

He turns to me, trembling. 'So you bloody should, Indie,' he says in a low, broken voice. 'I thought you loved me.'

I fling myself at him. 'I'm sorry,' I sob, over and over again, and at last his arms come round me and we cling to each other like two drowning souls.

'I'll never doubt you again,' I promise and he does a sort of choked-up laugh, deep in his throat.

'You will,' he says. 'You should. You know what I'm like. You were right, you know. I never paid that fine. I just told you I had to stop you worrying.'

'It doesn't matter.'

'I will pay it.'

'I know you will. And I'm going to help you.'

'No, it's my problem, not yours . . .'

I stop his protests with a kiss. 'It's mine too. I love you, Rick. We're a couple.'

'I love you too.'

There's a moan. Followed by a painful, high-pitched, keening sound. We turn in surprise as Scarlett's legs buckle beneath her. I'd forgotten she was there. She slips to the floor and buries her face in her hands, sobs tearing through her body.

'Scarlett, what is it?' I ask, kneeling down beside her.

'I'm sorry!' she howls.

Rick snorts in derision. 'Don't listen to her! Bloody drama queen.'

'It's all my fault!' she sobs. 'I shouldn't have interfered.'

'No, you bloody shouldn't,' he agrees, and she howls even louder.

'Scarlett?' I say, pulling her hands away from her face. 'Look at me. What is it? What's all this about?'

Scarlett stops yelling and looks up at me sorrowfully. 'I was jealous if you must know,' she admits. 'Isn't it obvious? I've got nobody. And you two – you're so good together. It's not fair!'

She sounds about twelve and for all the fuss she's

177

making there's barely a tear in sight. Rick glares at her and she sniffs mournfully. The situation is becoming ridiculous. It's like being back in the playground, playing piggy-in-the-middle with these two. I bite my lip, suddenly feeling an overwhelming desire to giggle. Scarlett stares at me in surprise. 'It's not funny!' she says resentfully and I can't help it, I burst out laughing. She reminds me of a cross little hedgehog rolled up in a ball, her spikes protecting the vulnerable little creature she is inside.

'What are you like? Come here!' I grab her by the hand and pull her to her feet. 'There's no need to be jealous, idiot. We love you too, don't we, Rick?'

'Um . . .' says my boyfriend, and looks so alarmed it makes Scarlett giggle too. I seize my opportunity and put my arms round them both.

'You two need to grow up and get to know each other properly,' I say firmly. 'It's time you made up.'

'So did things get better after that?'

'In some ways. Rick made an effort, and so did Scarlett, and after a while they started to get on. I mean, it was surprising he took against her in the first place. Normally Rick gets on with everyone.

'But there was still the problem of the missing money. I got on to the bank but they wouldn't listen. They said the money had been taken out from my normal cash machine – the one at college – and as far as they were concerned everything was fine. Which left me three hundred pounds down.'

'Three hundred pounds? That's a lot of money.'

'Yep! It was six weeks' work for me! I was broke. And poor Rick was worse off than me. He still had a five-hundred-quid fine to pay.'

'So what did you do?'

'Worked our bloody socks off.

'And Rick sold his car.'

22

Rick asked his boss for a pay-rise. His boss told him in no uncertain terms where to go. But he did say he could work Sundays as well and he wouldn't put it through the books. Rick was made up.

'Won't take me long to pay that fine now!'

Ever the optimist.

First chance I got, I asked Gordon for a pay-rise too.

'Sorry Indie, I wish I could. But I've got Scarlett's wages to find, now I've taken her on, and times are hard, you don't need me to tell you that.'

No, I don't. I swallow hard and ask him for more hours instead.

'When?'

'Sundays? I could come in on Sundays.' I might as well. If Rick was working I wouldn't be able to see him anyway.

'Indie, the shop's not open on Sundays,' he points out patiently.

'I know that. But it could be.' Even to me I sound desperate.

He shakes his head. 'No one wants their hair done on a Sunday.'

'How about late-night opening then on the run up to Christmas? You know how busy we get. If I came in after college each day, you could fit in some more clients.'

He starts to look interested. 'That's an idea. But can you manage that sort of workload plus your college work as well?'

Daddy Gordon. He's always taken a fatherly interest in my course, unlike some work-placement employers.

'It's fine.'

I needed this extra income. I was broke, Christmas was coming and I was desperate to help Rick out with his fine after I'd let him down so badly. My course was going to have to take a back-seat for a while. Just till we got straight.

'OK. Just till Christmas then. You can come in at four every day till we close. Starting Monday.'

'Four?'

'Yes. Is that a problem?' He's watching me closely. I can't let him change his mind.

'Not at all.' But it is. It means I would have to miss the

last session of the day. Every day. And at the end of term I had some practical tests coming up. Well, I would just have to cross that bridge when I came to it.

Shazza is mad at me. 'Why did you ask him to stay open later?' she says furiously, first chance she gets. 'He'll expect me to stay on too.'

'No, he won't. Anyway, I need the money, isn't it obvious?'

'If he hadn't given that Scarlett a job, we could all have had a pay-rise instead.'

That Scarlett. Surprising the dislike you can convey in such an innocent little word. Unlike the rest of the crew, I don't think Shazza is a fan of the new girl. I'm not surprised. Even though Shazza's been working for a few years, she's nowhere near as efficient as Scarlett. Increasingly I've noticed Gordon's been getting Scarlett to do the shampooing and booking appointments while Shazza's been relegated to the more menial tasks such as sweeping up. Shazza's pretty little nose has been put out of joint.

Today it's fairly quiet in the salon. Only Gordon and we three juniors are in. I'm doing a trim, Scarlett is tidying up, Shaz is sitting by the desk, filing her nails and looking bored out of her skull. She's never really got it that you should try to look busy even if you're not. Gordon is doing a colour on one of his older clients.

'Can you mix a 7 with a 7NA for Mrs Rowe, Shaz?' he calls, but he's too late, I've just seen her disappear outside for a quick smoke. Gordon would go mad if he knew.

'She's not here,' says Scarlett.

'Where is she?' says Gordon testily.

'Gone to the loo,' I butt in quickly, before Scarlett puts her foot in it.

'I'll give her a knock,' says Scarlett. Then she's back with a puzzled look on her face and before I can stop her she says, 'She's not there either. She must've nipped out for a fag.'

Scarlett! Why doesn't she think?

Gordon mutters under his breath, something to the effect of Shazza never being around when she's needed.

'I can do that for you,' Scarlett offers. 'I've just done basic colour-mixing at college.'

'Are you sure?' says Gordon and she says, 'Of course,' and trips off in her high heels to fetch Mrs Rowe's colour card like she's done it millions of times before.

When Shazza sneaks back in, Gordon looks up and says curtly, 'Clean the basins, Sharon, then sweep up please,' and after that he keeps Scarlett as his assistant and gives all the boring jobs to Shazza to do instead.

By the end of the day the normally bouncy, bubbly Shazza is totally fed up – and it shows.

'Good work, Scarlett,' says Gordon. 'You're coming on a treat. You'll be running the salon soon at this rate. You can go now. Sharon, put the towels on to wash before you leave.'

Shazza flounces off to the staff room with an armful of wet towels and a scowl on her face while Scarlett comes over to the desk where I'm counting out the tips.

'That was great!' she says. 'I feel like I've learned loads today. Any of those for me?'

'Three-way split,' I say. 'You know the score, Gordon lets you, me and Shaz divide the tips between us. It's been pretty quiet today. Twenty quid, that's all.'

She sniffs. 'That's ten for you and ten for me then.'

'Uh? What about Shazza?'

'Get lost! She didn't do anything, did she? 'Cept hang around all day with a face like a slapped backside. You and me, we worked non-stop.'

'It doesn't work like that.'

'Well it should. You want to toughen up a bit, girl.' She counts out ten pounds and shoves it in her pocket. 'I'm out of here. See ya!'

'Scarlett!' I protest but she pushes past Shazza, who's on her way back in, ignoring her completely, and shouts

185

breezily back at me, 'See you at home, yeah?'

That girl is a law unto herself. Shaz looks daggers at her retreating back.

'How do you put up with her at home as well as work?' she asks.

'Oh, Scarlett's all right once you get to know her,' I say, but Shaz doesn't look convinced.

'Has she got a bloke?'

'Not that I know of. I don't think she wants one.'

'Huh! That's what she says. Have you got my tips?' she says, changing the subject. I sigh heavily and divide what's left between us.

'Not much today,' she says, glumly staring at the small number of coins in her hand.

No, not much at all, thanks to Scarlett. I'm never going to clear Rick's debts this way.

23

As the weeks go by I start to think that Scarlett may have a boyfriend after all. She hasn't said anything and I don't want to pry, but she's spending more and more time out of the house and seems far less dependent on me. She's spending more time on her appearance too, which is always a sure-fire sign there's a bloke in tow. I wonder who he is. He can't be from college or I'd know it.

She still copies me, but there's an edge to her now. We are so similar to look at, everyone comments on it, but it's almost as if most people have forgotten that I was Version One. The other day I got mistaken for her by someone at college!

'Can you believe it?' I grumble to Mel, feeling quite aggrieved for some obscure reason.

'Well, you are pretty alike,' she says, and it's as if she of all people can't remember either that I came first. After all the fuss she made about Scarlett being a copycat! Then she makes it even worse by saying, 'But anyone who knows you can see that you're two completely different people.'

'*He* didn't!'

'Yeah, but if he knew you properly he would. Like, with you, what you see is what you get whereas with Scarlett, I don't know, there's something different about her. Something raw, edgy, subversive . . .'

I stare at her, offended. 'Oh, I see. So we're identical twins only I'm the boring one and she's the exciting one . . .'

'I never said that!' protests Mel.

No, but she meant it all right. Even Mel seems to have changed her tune about Scarlett, who spends more time with the girls than I do nowadays. She gets to hang out with them in the common room while I'm in the library catching up on work I've missed because I'm always at the salon. All right for some.

I don't know what's the matter with me. I never used to be this grouchy.

Actually, I do. I'm fed up to be honest. My whole life is work, work, work. I'm either at college or the salon, and all for Rick's fine. It's hard going. I'm at Herr Cutz every single night, and I'm trying to keep up with my course, and I'm worrying about skipping lectures – which someone is going to notice sooner or later – and all in all I'm feeling stressed out of my head!

Worst of all, I hardly get to see Rick any more. He works on Sundays, which is my only day off! Oh well, at least it means we're not spending any money.

It will be worth it in the end, I tell myself.

But then – just when I think things can't get much worse – they do.

It's a dark, wet, windy night and I've worked late at the salon. As I come out I spot a couple across the road, huddled together in the doorway of the pub opposite, sheltering from the rain. I hardly give them a second glance, I'm too intent on seeing if a bus is coming. Not for the first time I wish Rick still had his licence and could pick me up on a night like this in his nice warm car. But then, if he still had his licence I wouldn't be working at night to pay off his fine in the first place, would I?

Then someone shouts 'Indie!' and it's him. He's waving at me from the doorway and now I'm confused. Rick's got a girl with him. Who is it?

He runs over to me with the girl trailing behind and now I can see it's Scarlett. What are they doing together?

But it's OK, they're both grinning, they're pleased to see me. There's nothing wrong.

Of course there's nothing wrong. What am I afraid of?

'What are you doing here?'

'Got some news for you,' says Rick. 'Don't worry, it's good news. Let's go for a drink.'

'You've been drinking already,' I say. 'I can smell it on your breath.'

'Got something to celebrate,' he says.

We make our way into the steamy, crowded pub and Scarlett and I find a seat while Rick battles his way to the bar.

'What's all this about?' I ask, but she just grins and shakes her head.

'It's Rick's news, not mine.'

So how come she knows about it before I do? This is so annoying. I wait impatiently till Rick comes back with the drinks.

'Go on then! I can't stand it any more. What have you done now?'

A pained expression flits over Rick's face.

'Sorry!' I say immediately. 'Didn't mean it like that. Bit tired, that's all. Been a long day.'

'Don't worry,' he says, good humour instantly restored. 'This will cheer you up.'

'What?'

'I've sold my car.'

'Really?' I let out my breath in a long sigh. I hadn't even realized I was holding it. 'That's brilliant!' His smile widens. But then I can't resist adding, 'How much?'

'Enough.'

'That's awesome, Rick.' I mean it. I know what a sacrifice that must have been for him.

'So, now you can jack your extra hours in if you like. You said you're knackered.'

'Or give them to me,' offers Scarlett. 'I'll do them for you.'

I hesitate. I'm not too sure about handing over more hours to her. Exhausted though I am, at the end of this course I still want a full-time job at Herr Cutz. And if I start messing Gordon around, he might have second thoughts. So I say, 'We'll see. How did this come about, Rick?'

'It's all thanks to Scarlett. She made me see sense.'

I glance at her and she smiles smugly back at me. 'We were in here waiting for you and I just said to him, what's the point in having a Triumph Herald sitting in the garage if you can't drive it? Might as well sell it and pay off your debts.'

Like that thought hadn't occurred to me? The difference

191

was, I wouldn't ask him to do it. I knew how much having a car meant to him. Especially that little Triumph. Anyway, who was she to give advice to *my* boyfriend on how to run his life? Irritation crawls over me like a swarm of ants and then the questions come thick and fast, nipping, biting, tormenting me.

When did they start going out for a drink together? When did she start doling out the advice? When did he start listening to her? And if I'd suggested it, would he have listened to me?

Rick takes up the story. 'Then this guy turns round and says, "Excuse me mate, couldn't help overhearing. Have you got a Triumph Herald for sale?" And it turns out he's been looking for one for ages. So we get talking and in the end, he buys it off me!'

Simple as that. To be honest, I can't get over how well he's taken parting with it. He's still grinning broadly at me, like he's won the lottery instead of losing his pride and joy. Maybe I should stop begrudging Scarlett and be grateful for her good influence on Rick.

Maybe pigs can fly. As I try my best to be generous and return their self-satisfied smiles, his next words bring me back down to earth with a bump.

'But the beauty is, Ind, I've not just sold my car, I've gained one too.'

Alarm bells start ringing in my head. 'What d'you mean?'

'I've done like a part-exchange. This guy wanted the Triumph so much he gave me more than enough to clear my fine and threw in his wheels as well.'

'His wheels?'

'He was driving an old nineteen-sixties American Chevrolet. I can't believe it. Needs a fair bit of work on it mind, but once I've done it up and it's taxed and insured, I reckon it'll be worth a bit.'

'You've bought a car that's not even roadworthy?'

'I didn't buy it! I told you, I got it for nothing. And I'm not going to drive it.' A note of irritation has crept into his voice but then he smiles at me again, trying to appease me. He's like a kid, wanting my approval. 'Well, I can't, can I? Not yet. I'm going to do it up and sell it on. It's an investment.'

I stare at him, trying to make sense of Rick's logic in my head. It sounded OK. And if anyone could do it, he could, I had no doubt about that. Rick was a superb mechanic. The best. But I still wasn't convinced.

'Come and have a look,' he says, knocking back his drink and getting to his feet.

'Where is it?'

'Round my place. The guy drove me home to see the

Triumph and he did the deal there and then. We swapped cars and he gave me a nice little cheque as well. Look.'

He takes a cheque out of his pocket and thrusts it into my hand. My eyes widen. It's loads more than I thought it would be. Maybe this makes sense after all.

We jump into a taxi and head over to Rick's place. Outside the house stands a massive beaten-up wreck of a car. Bizarrely, it appears to me almost lifelike: its headlights are eyes, staring at me; a badge of some kind is a squashed nose; a grill stretches from one side to the other in a wide, vacant leer. It's like a battered, punch-drunk old fighter, way past its prime. Rick strokes the bonnet lovingly.

'There you go, old-timer,' he says, his voice hushed and tender. He turns to me, his eyes shining. 'Isn't that the coolest thing you've ever seen?'

I don't have the heart to tell him otherwise.

24

It didn't occur to me straight away. I wasn't exactly thrilled that Rick had acquired yet another car, but let's face it, he was never going to be without one, was he? And at least now he could pay off his fine. The pressure was off us at last and we could ease up on all the extra work we'd taken on and get on with our lives.

Rick wanted to drive us home in the Chevvie but I wouldn't let him. For a start he'd been drinking, though he swore he wasn't over the limit. But there was still the small matter of no licence.

In the end, Scarlett and I go home in a taxi and leave him alone drooling over the new car in his life.

I go straight to bed, I'm worn out, but I can't sleep. I'm tossing and turning all night long, my head in a whirl. Something is bugging me and I don't know what it is. I'm still a bit peeved that Scarlett appears much more in the know about my boyfriend's affairs than I am, but it's more than that. Something else isn't right . . .

I must've dropped off for a while eventually because suddenly I wake up and sit bolt upright, my heart thudding.

I know what's wrong. But still, I have to check it out. I leap out of bed, switch on my computer and go on the internet. My heart sinks.

There it is in black and white. If you buy a car on a credit agreement, it belongs to the finance company. If you sell it, you still have to pay any outstanding finance that remains.

Would Rick have remembered that?

Would he have even known it in the first place?

No chance. Rick is not the sort of person to check the fine print. The only thing I have ever seen him reading all the time we've been together is a car manual.

'That's my fine paid,' he'd boasted. 'And all my debts cleared. We're laughing.'

I'm not laughing now. I feel like screaming with frustration. I don't know what it is about my boyfriend. He just seems to lurch from one crisis to the next. Being with him is like being on a roller coaster, all highs and lows, twisting and turning, hanging on by your fingertips for grim death before you take another leap into the unknown. A tap on my door makes me jump.

'Saw your light on.' Scarlett's head appears round the door. 'Can't you sleep?'

'Look at this.'

Scarlett frowns and moves to my side, peering at the screen. As she scrolls down the information her eyes widen. 'Uh-oh! I never knew that, did you?'

'Rick didn't, that's for sure. He thinks he doesn't have to make those payments any more. We need to get the car back. Who did he sell it to?'

She shrugs. 'Dunno. Just some random guy in the pub.'

My blood runs cold and I grab my phone. 'I need to speak to him. Now.'

But his phone is switched off and I have to wait till he swaggers into college next morning, before I can have a word. His fingernails are black with oil and it's pretty obvious what he's been up to.

He's as happy as a sand-boy, whatever a sand-boy is, and, as usual, it's me that has to spoil it.

'What d'you mean, I still have to repay the loan every month?' he says blankly. 'That's not fair.'

'It's the law, Rick.'

'But he owns the car now, not me.'

'*He* doesn't. The finance company do. You should've known this. What's his name anyway?'

'Scott.'

'What's his other name?'

'I dunno. Scott Something.'

'You'd better find out. Because you need to buy it back from him quick before they discover what you've done.'

'But – don't let's be hasty. What if I do have to make the repayments myself? It's still a good deal, Ind. I've got the money to pay my fine and I can pay back the loan out of my wages.'

I knew it. He'd done it again, I could read all the signs. My boyfriend had fallen head over heels in love with yet another heap of old metal. I grit my teeth.

'Rick, you have sold something that doesn't belong to you. It's a criminal offence. You could go to prison. You need to find this guy, return the car and his cheque to him and get your own car back.'

He looks a bit sheepish. 'I can't do that.'

'Why not?'

'I've already paid it into my account.'

'Shit! Rick, you have to find him. Tell him to stop the cheque, it won't be cleared yet. Get the Triumph back. And give him back that pile of crap!' My instructions, rattled out like machine-gun fire, come to a halt as his face darkens.

'Don't tell me what I can and can't do.'

Mistake. I've insulted the new love of his life.

'Rick, this is serious. You have got to get the car back. You have got to find him.'

'I know! I will, all right? I'll go back to the pub tonight. I'll sort it. Now, get off my back!'

He thrusts his hands into his pockets and walks away from me, shoulders hunched. I feel terrible, snatching away his happiness like this.

Is it always going to be like this between us?

He avoids me all day but late afternoon I see him and Scarlett walking out of college together. I run after them. 'Where are you two off to?'

They turn around and Rick scowls at me. 'Where d'you think? To find that guy.' His voice is truculent, like he's blaming me for all this.

'Wait, I'll come with you.'

'No need, shouldn't take long. Even if he's not in the pub, someone'll know who he is. He said he was a regular.'

'You've got your job to go to,' says Scarlett. 'I'll go with him.'

'I'll call in sick,' I say, not liking the way she's muscling in. 'I can help. Explain to the guy why you've had to change your mind. Say you didn't know.'

'Yeah, 'cos I'm too thick to realize,' he says bitterly. But then he adds, 'Come if you want.'

Gordon is surprised when I cry off work. I've never done it before in over a year of working for him. 'I've got a sore throat,' I lie on the phone. 'And a headache.' I cough once or twice for good measure. 'I think I might be coming down with flu.'

'Hot honey and lemon,' he says immediately, 'and an early night. Don't worry about a thing, Indie, we'll manage. Look after yourself, darling.'

I hate lying to someone like Gordon. Someone nice and kind and good. Someone who trusts me.

Scarlett is looking at me with respect. 'You're a good liar,' she says.

That's the sort of compliment that only makes you feel worse.

25

The pub is almost empty at this time of day, just a few solitary drinkers propping up the bar, plus a handful outside on the pavement, smoking and arguing about the state of the world. I think I recognize the guy behind the bar but otherwise there's no resemblance between last night's lively venue and this gloomy mausoleum. An air of quiet desperation hangs over the dark interior like a lingering cloud of the cigarette smoke that has now been banned.

'Scott? Can't say I know anyone called Scott,' says the barman in response to Rick's question. 'Hey, Dezzy, you know someone called Scott? These guys are looking for him.'

A man at the end of the bar shakes his head and thrusts his glass forward. 'Same again.'

'Paddy?'

'Never heard of him.'

'John? You heard of a guy called Scott?' John doesn't bother to reply. The state he's in, I'd doubt he'd recognize his own mother if she was sitting next to him.

'Big guy. Shaved head. South London accent,' Rick persists. The barman chuckles.

'That just about describes every second bloke we get in here.'

'Wearing a leather jacket,' says Rick, starting to look desperate.

'Looked like he could take care of himself,' chips in Scarlett.

The guy shrugs, his face a tad wary now. She shouldn't have said that, even if it's true. Especially if it's true. He wasn't going to look for trouble. 'I should hang about for a bit, see if he comes in. Can I get you a drink?'

We sit there the three of us. All night. Watching the door. If one of us gets up to go to the bar or the toilet, the others keep vigil. The pub fills up slowly and the barman is right, every second guy who walks through those doors could more or less answer Scott's description – but none of them is him. As the night wears on and the pub gets packed again, we consume more alcohol, but if it's meant to be a relaxant, it's clearly not working. Beside me I can feel the tension radiating off Rick like the beam from a lighthouse. When time is called, he looks so sick, I think he's going to throw up.

We stumble out of the doors into the cold night air.

'This might be harder than I thought,' mumbles Rick.

'We'll come back tomorrow,' I say comfortingly.

'And the next night and the one after that and the one after that, until we find him,' adds Scarlett, and I find myself squeezing his arm possessively as he manages a weak smile at her.

And we do. Rick and I do, I mean. Not Scarlett.

Because the next day, when I'm about to ring in to tell Gordon I've still got the flu and I'll be off indefinitely, she offers to do my hours for me instead.

'Only we don't both need to be there holding Rick's hand – and he is *your* boyfriend,' she says. 'And I could really do with the money.'

So could I! I think savagely, but let's face it, he *is* my problem, not hers. I put it to Gordon and he says 'Yes!' like she's saved his life. So everyone's happy. Except me.

'Don't you go telling Gordon I'm faking it!' I warn her, remembering how she'd blurted out to him that Shazza had nipped out for a fag.

'Like I would!' she says.

So the next night it's just me and Rick sitting there nursing our drinks, our eyes glued to that door.

And the one after that.

'This is pointless,' says Rick after we've spent our third consecutive night in the pub. 'I'll probably never see him again. I give up.'

'You can't!' I say, fighting the panic that's rising in my throat.

'Indie! It's not that bad. OK, I made a bad decision. But I've still got a motor and I've got money now to pay the fine and I can keep up the payments out of my wages. It's no big deal!'

I sigh heavily as we walk home together through the empty streets. I wish I had Rick's optimism. Me, I'm more a glass half empty kind of girl. I can still see problems down the line and they're threatening to choke me.

'But Rick, think about it. What if this Scott bloke sells the car on? Or you default on the payments? Or the finance company find out what you've done? Or what if—'

'Shh.' Rick stops and draws me close to him. 'Stop worrying, Indie. I won't default on the payments and none of that stuff will happen. Don't stress about problems which aren't even there. Trust me.'

I lay my cheek against his chest and feel myself relax. His strong arms are around me, his chin is resting on my head and I feel warm, safe, protected. His calm acceptance of the situation comforts me. Everything will be all right.

Rick's got his faults but he's a good guy. I love him. And Love conquers all, so they say.

That's what I really believed.

Then.

26

The next day we discover that the cheque has bounced.

Rick is totally beside himself. I've never seen him so angry. His language is unprintable and the things he says he's going to do to this bloke – well, let's not go there.

'Go to the police!' I say, but he scowls at me as though it's all my fault.

'How can I?' he explodes. 'Like you pointed out, I'm the one who's committed a criminal offence, selling him the car in the first place! How could I have been so flaming stupid?'

'You didn't know,' I say, but then Scarlett pipes up with, 'Ignorance is no excuse in the eyes of the law,' and we both know she's right. We're on one steep learning curve here.

I think Rick is more mad at himself than anyone else.

He doesn't want anyone to know what he's done, he feels such an idiot.

'I can't believe I gave my Triumph away to someone in a pub,' he groans. 'I loved that car.'

'There are a lot of criminals out there,' says Scarlett. 'At least you've still got the Chevvie.' But Rick is inconsolable, he wants the Triumph back.

He goes to the pub night after night, but it's no good. Scott has disappeared off the face of the earth. And now Rick's got a real problem. His fine is due to be paid up in full in a few days' time and we're both skint.

He asks his boss at the garage for an advance on his wages but his boss tells him where to go.

On Saturday, back at work again, I try Gordon instead, thinking he'll be a little more understanding.

'Please Gordon, just this once. I don't like to ask but I need to do my Christmas shopping, you see.'

'No, I don't see,' says Gordon sharply, and I stare at him in surprise. 'How do I know you'll make it in every day between now and Christmas, Indigo? You've already let me down this week.'

I have to stop myself from gasping aloud. This is so unlike him. I'd noticed he'd been a bit cool with me as soon as I'd set foot in the salon but I'd assumed it was because he was busy. But this was something else.

'I didn't let you down,' I protest, stung to the core. 'I had the flu, you know that.'

'Yeah, so you said. Well, you never know, you just might *have the flu* again and leave me in the lurch.'

He didn't believe me, he thought I was making it up. Well, I was. My cheeks flame. But how did he know that?

My eyes move to Scarlett, but she's intent on combing through a client's wet hair. She's quick and efficient, and when she's finished she smiles and says, 'There we are, Mrs Jenkins, Linda will be with you in a minute. Can I get you anything? Magazine? Cup of tea? Milk and two sugars, isn't it?'

I start to follow her out to the kitchen but Gordon says curtly, 'Indigo, tidy up round here please.' Then he turns to a woman waiting with a little boy and says, 'Scarlett will cut Zac's hair for you today, Mrs Smith. She won't be a minute. It'll save you waiting for Kay.'

My mouth drops open. It should be me cutting Zac's hair, not Scarlett, I've done it before. She won't even know what to do, even though it's quite simple, just a dry trim. I don't know what's going on round here, but one thing's pretty obvious, I'm not Gordon's blue-eyed girl any more. That honour seems to have been passed on to Scarlett.

As I swish my cloth balefully round the basins, Shazza smiles at me sympathetically. If anyone knows how I feel, she does. To make matters worse, I can't help but notice that Scarlett does know what to do after all. She's cutting Zac's hair with careful competence, concentrating on the task in hand, but chatting away to the little lad at the same time, keeping him happy. I recognize Gordon's touch. He's been teaching her. And she's good.

I feel myself seething quietly. At last she finishes – and the kid looks cute. Mrs Smith goes into raptures about what a good job she's done and Gordon looks on approvingly. When she pays me at the desk she leaves a ten-pound tip for Scarlett, more than she's ever given me.

Shazza sidles over to me. 'See *her*!' she says out of the corner of her mouth, nodding meaningfully at Scarlett. '*She* let the cat out of the bag you were skiving.'

'Did she?' I'm shocked. I never really thought Scarlett would do something like that to me. So that explained the way Gordon was behaving.

'Don't think she meant to,' admits Shaz. 'Gordon asked how you were and she just said fine. She said you were at the pub with Rick. She was busy at the time, not thinking. Then when she realized what she'd said she tried to cover up but it was too late.'

'Sharon and Indigo, can you stop chatting and find something to do?' says Gordon curtly, and I grab stray towels and fling them in the basket ready for washing.

Then I make a start on tidying the stock cupboard and, all the time, inside I'm blazing. Scarlett should be doing this, not me, but instead Gordon's giving her all the jobs I'd normally get to do. Colour-mixing, neutralizing, even the occasional trim. It's not fair. Meanwhile the tips continue to mount up for her in the blue porcelain pot.

At the end of the day I get to count them out. Wow, the most responsible job I've done all day, it's pathetic.

I'm not proud of what I do next – but I'm angry, with a slow-burning resentment that has been smouldering inside me all day. That's my excuse. I feel like Scarlett has stolen my job – and my reputation.

I divide up the tips as normal between the three of us. It's only fair, that's the way we've always done it, even though today it's actually Scarlett that's earned them all. It's quite a sum, the girl's done well.

I make three equal piles of one- and two-pound coins mainly, plus some silver and the odd generous fiver. Then I slip the ten-pound note that Mrs Smith left for Scarlett into my pocket.

She'd do the same. I'd seen her do it. But I never thought I would. Desperate times call for desperate measures.

It's not for me, it's for Rick. He needs it more than she does.

On Sunday night, he comes round to see me after work. Mum, Scarlett and I are all in the front room with my sister. The room is full of store bags. She'd called in on the way home from an early Christmas shopping expedition and we're all drooling over the generous purchases she's made.

'What did you get me?' I ask and Tamsyn grins and says, 'Wait and see, greedy clogs.' But the truth is, I'm hoping she hasn't spent a lot on me because no one will be getting much from me this year, that's for sure.

When Rick arrives I shut the door firmly on them and leave them to it. As we go upstairs to my bedroom their voices, loud and laughing, float up after us.

'Scarlett's practically one of the family now,' I observe, inviting discussion. Because, I'm not too sure how I feel about this. But Rick ignores my comment. He seems preoccupied, like he's got the weight of the world on his shoulders. At last he speaks.

'My fine's due tomorrow.'

'How much have you got?'

He grunts, pulling an envelope containing his wages out of his back pocket. Then he empties his side pockets of change.

'That much.'

I take my purse out of my bag and count out the notes, including Scarlett's tenner. Then I upend the purse so all the coins spill out on the floor.

'And that much.'

'No, Indie, I can't take all your money . . .'

'Yes you can,' I say firmly. 'You've got to. You don't have any choice.'

He sighs and takes my face in his hands, staring unblinkingly into my eyes.

'I will pay you back, every penny, I swear.'

'I know you will.'

But when we count it all up, it's still not enough. Rick flops down on my bed and for the first time he looks scared. 'I'm still a hundred quid short.'

'We could ask my mum and dad to help,' I say quietly, but his face hardens.

'No way! If my own father won't help me, I'm not going to ask yours to bail me out.' Poor Rick. He's never had the advantages I have. 'Your dad thinks I'm a jerk already,' he adds under his breath.

I didn't realize he was so aware of my dad's opinion of him. It's heartbreaking. Rick tries so hard and he's a really good worker, not like his dad at all, but my father is all too ready to tar him with the same brush.

And now he's going to get into trouble for not paying

his fine and justify all my dad's prejudices.

I take a deep breath. 'I'll go and make you a cup of coffee and we'll sort this out,' I say, but he doesn't even bother to reply.

Downstairs, I put the kettle on. Loud laughter emanates from the front room where the shopping fest presentation is still underway. People waste money on crap nowadays, I think bitterly, Tamsyn must be made of money. I feel like marching into that room and asking her or my mum outright for help, but something stops me. I can't do it. I can't do it to Rick. He'd hate me for it. And I can't do it to myself. Not in front of Scarlett. I'm too proud.

Pride comes before a fall, so they say.

Tamsyn's bag is where she left it on the hall table. Her wallet is poking out of it. Bet she's got no money left. My fingers slip inside to investigate and feel notes folded over on themselves. I don't even look, I just slide them out and stuff them in my back pocket.

And then the front room door opens and Mum is standing there.

'You made me jump!' I say. Then I add glibly, 'Kettle's boiled. Just came to see if you want a cup of coffee.'

27

I tell him it's money I've put aside for Christmas.

'No!' he says. 'You can't do that!'

I thrust it into his hands. 'Yes I can. Call it an early Christmas present. You're not getting anything else, that's for sure.'

'You're the best present I could ever have,' he says and kisses me gratefully.

The next day he pays his fine in full and I breathe a huge sigh of relief.

'I'll meet you after work tonight,' he says, the smile back on his face for the first time for ages. 'We'll go somewhere to celebrate.'

The last thing I feel like is celebrating. I've stolen from my own sister and I hate myself for it, plus now I've got the difficult, almost impossible, task of replacing the money before she discovers what I've done. At least I've had a slight reprieve. When Dave came to collect her last night she went off home dizzy with all her purchases and left her handbag on the table. Later on she rang us in a panic, afraid she'd lost it out shopping. When she knew it was safe with us (Safe? Ha ha! I feel so guilty!) Tams asked us to hang on to it till she could collect it later in the week. So I've got away with it. So far.

'Where *can* we go that doesn't cost anything?' I say glumly and his face falls.

But he thinks for a while and then says, 'I know just the place. Don't worry about a thing.'

Why is it when Rick tells me not to worry it has the opposite effect on me?

'Don't go wasting any money, Rick!' I warn him sternly and he holds his hands up, displaying his empty palms.

'I haven't got any to waste!'

That evening at work Gordon isn't so frosty with me like he was on Saturday, he's more or less back to normal. Maybe it's because blue-eyed Scarlett isn't around. Or maybe he has to use my skills tonight whether he likes it or not because it's just the two of us on. Anyway, it's nice to be working alongside him again properly. I hated that feeling that I couldn't be trusted. That's not me.

At the end of the evening he says, 'Thanks a bunch, Indie darling, you've been a star!' and then he winks at me. 'Great idea of yours, late-night opening. I can see you running your own successful salon one day,' and I go out into the cold night air glowing. OK, I cocked up, but all is not lost. I'll put everything right. I'll replace Tam's money somehow, even if I have to get a bleeding bank loan, and then everything will be as it was and I will never, ever, ever do anything wrong again in my whole life!

And outside, waiting for me on the pavement, irresistible as ever, is my lovely boy and he's holding a single red rose.

'Don't have a go at me,' he says anxiously, 'it didn't cost much.'

'It's perfect!' I say, reaching up to kiss him. 'Didn't you know? Less is more nowadays.'

We walk through the dark streets, our arms wrapped round each other. 'Where are we going?' I ask.

But he just smiles mysteriously and says, 'Hungry?'

I nod because I'm starving but then immediately add, 'We can't go out for dinner, Rick!' and he laughs.

'*We can't go out for dinner, Rick!*' he parodies, his voice an absurdly high take-off of mine, and I punch him in the ribs but I can't help laughing too.

We pass through a down-at-heel high street full of charity shops, cash-converters, off-licences and take-aways. 'Here we are!' he says and comes to a halt outside a particularly grubby-looking kebab shop. Through the greasy window where a dead fly is trapped in the corner, I can see an unappetizing lump of meat, dripping with fat, turning slowly on a spit. My heart sinks. Serves me right. Maybe now is the time to turn vegetarian.

But as I put my foot on the step, determined to put a brave face on things, Rick bursts out laughing again.

'Had you!' he says and I scream.

'Rick! I'm going to get you!'

'Got to catch me first!' he yells and runs off down the street.

I chase after him, yelling, 'Cheat! Rick, wait for me!' but he disappears around the corner. And as I charge around it he's there with his arms out, waiting for me and I run slap, bang into them,.

He picks me up and spins me round then comes to a stop, looking down at me, his face serious.

'I love you, Indigo Moore,' he says.

'I love you too, Richard Thomas,' I say solemnly, and we kiss.

And afterwards he takes me home to his place for dinner.

* * *

I've never actually been inside Rick's house before, though I did make it to the garage on one memorable occasion. It's always been sort of understood between us that he didn't want to take me there. I guess, like my dad, he thought it was the wrong side of the tracks or something. That makes me sound like a snob too, but nothing could be further from the truth. It was his decision, not mine, and I respected it.

He lives on a big sprawling estate, the kind that has gardens with the front wall removed, littered with old cars, broken-down washing machines and abandoned kids' toys. I mean toys that have been abandoned, not kids, though there may have been one or two of those on that estate too.

His house, a pebble-dashed semi, is identical to the rest of the houses in the street, but was immediately identifiable to me by the beaten-up Chevvie sprawling by the front door.

I hesitate, suddenly nervous. 'Anyone in?'

He shakes his head. 'Mum's at work.'

I remembered then that his mum worked nights, cleaning offices.

'You won't see my dad till after chucking-out time and

I bribed our Marnie to take Kylie and Craig for the night. The coast is clear!'

I smile, glad that Rick's sister – whom I recall had recently moved in with her latest boyfriend – had relieved me of the pressure of meeting Rick's younger siblings for the first time.

He inserts the key and we step inside.

It's a bit stuffy and the smell of cooked food lingers in the air. The hallway is a dumping ground for coats, bags, shoes and keys, but that's nothing out of the ordinary. Rick ushers me into a long, narrow room with laminated flooring and a mismatch of chairs and sofas which are lined up opposite a huge, wall-mounted television screen. My first impression is it's pretty bare, but then I spot that someone has gathered together the detritus of family living – toys, clothes, junk-mail, the lot – and stuffed them behind the sofa. The wallpaper is a tad scuffed and torn, and I know what my mum would say, there's not a book in sight. But there's nothing to be ashamed of here.

Why hadn't he brought me here before? I blink, suppressing the urge to cry. Is Rick's opinion of me so low that he thought I'd object to his home just because it didn't have all the creature comforts mine has? Does he really think I'm that shallow?

Then I catch sight of a table at the far end of the room and gasp.

It's laid for two. In the centre someone has placed a narrow, long-stemmed white china vase and I know, intuitively, it's waiting for my rose. On either side two places have been set with matching plates, cutlery and glasses, a red paper serviette tucked artfully into each glass, a bottle of red wine standing between them, waiting to be opened.

It takes my breath away, that carefully laid table in the humdrum family room. It's just so simple. So tasteful. And it says so much.

Rick's done this. For me. After college he must've rushed around like a madman, cleaning, tidying up, shopping, cooking. It's the most romantic thing anyone has ever done for me.

Because he has cooked for me. Properly. It's not just a take-away. He's taken a lot of trouble to produce what he knows is my favourite meal.

He sits me down at the table and pours us both a glass of wine while he heats up the oriental beef and mushroom soup he's prepared earlier. It's delicious. After that we eat prawn and vegetable stir-fry which he cooks in front of me, the heat rising in a blue haze from his mum's frying pan as he deftly adds mange-tout, peppers, pak choi, cashew nuts and noodles to the meal. I am so impressed.

'I never even knew you could cook,' I say, forking the yummy food into my mouth.

'Just goes to show you don't know everything about me,' he grins, reaching for a can of lager. 'Want one?' he offers, but I shake my head. Then he adds, 'I do quite a bit of cooking for the family as it happens. I'm usually the one who makes the dinner if Mum's out at work.'

He's right. There is so much more to Rick than meets the eye. I wish my dad could see it too.

Afterwards we take what's left of the wine upstairs with us.

I was so happy.

I lapse into silence, remembering that night.

At the other end of the phone I can sense Mrs Moffat still there, listening. She's got the patience of a saint.

Mother Teresa was a saint. Not a sinner, like me.

'That was the last time.'

'The last time for what, Indie?'

'I was happy.' My voice is choked.

She waits. After a while she says gently, 'Did something happen that night?'

The tears spill over and I sob for my wrecked life. But I'm not alone any more. She's with me in the darkness, holding my hand.

'Do you want to tell me about it?'

'Yes.' I've got to tell someone. But the words won't come.

'Is it to do with Rick?'

'Yes.' Just a whisper floating down the phone, but she catches it.

'Tell me, Indie. Did he do something to you that night? Did Rick hurt you?'

Her words splash over me like a bucket of cold water, making me gasp, bringing me to my senses.

She doesn't understand. How could she?

'No,' I say. 'It wasn't like that. It was Rick who was hurt that night, not me.'

28

I'm half-asleep when I hear the sound of my phone ringing. Quickly, trying not to disturb Rick, I disentangle myself from his arm and dig it out of my bag.

'Who is it?' he murmurs drowsily.

'Scarlett.'

Groan.

'Where are you?' she asks.

'At Rick's.'

'Rick's?' she asks in surprise. 'What are you doing there?'

Mind your own business, I nearly say, but manage to refrain. 'What do you want?'

'Nothing. Only your mum's wondering if you're coming home for dinner.'

'Tell her I've already eaten. I'll be home in a couple of hours.'

Scarlett is beginning to get on my nerves. I need space from her, she's crowding me. 'See you later,' I say crisply and switch my phone off. Rick reaches for me and all thoughts of Scarlett disappear.

But eventually the fairytale has to come to an end and it's time to get up. I don't want Rick's dad coming home from the pub and walking in on us. Reluctantly we get dressed and, I remember now, I felt a bit awkward. Rick shares his bedroom with his kid brother, you see, and Batman paraphernalia was all round the room. Not exactly the right ambience for a big seduction scene. (Is it still seduction if you both want each other equally?)

We go downstairs to clear up and I'm grateful for the domestic stuff to cover up my sudden shyness. Rick is quiet too, like he doesn't know what to say, and I wonder if he's feeling as awkward as I do. It's not like it's the first time but now it seems a bit weird, getting it together in his house. Like he'd planned it all.

I cram the empty lager cans into the bin. Rick must've had more to drink than I thought.

When we've finished I say, bright and breezy, 'Better make myself scarce then,' and reach for my coat.

'I'll walk you home,' says Rick.

'No need, I can get a taxi.'

'I can't let you do that.'

What is wrong with us? We are acting like polite strangers to each other. Then Rick pulls a solemn face, the one he does sometimes to take me off, and wags a stern finger at me.

'Don't you know taxis are a waste of money?' he scolds, his voice exactly like mine, and as we both burst out laughing, the awkward spell is broken. He pulls on a hoody, chucks his keys in his pocket and holds out his hand. 'Come on, you. Maybe we'll go mad, hey, and get the bus?'

The stars were out as if someone had waved a magic wand and sprinkled them throughout the sky. It reminded me of that night on the beach back in the summer when life was simple and we'd been so happy. It seemed so long ago now, like another age. And there was a full moon. It was cold and frost glistened on the cracked pavements, the patchy grass and the roofs of parked cars, making the run-down estate look almost enchanting.

Funny the things you remember.

We stood outside on the pavement, arms round each other, gazing up at the night sky. I didn't want to go home, I wanted to stay with him forever. Middle-aged couples, on their way home from a night out, walked past us and smiled, huddling that bit closer to each other, as if we reminded them what it was like to be young and in love. If they only knew. With what we'd been through lately in some ways I felt as old as them.

Around us, even at that late hour, the estate teemed with life. Cats screeched, dogs barked and magically an urban fox slunk across the road in front of us. From the surrounding houses you could hear the sound of a baby crying, a television turned up too loud, the low, insistent pulse of music pounding from a teenage bedroom, two voices raised in anger. But we were at peace in our own little bubble of happiness.

I loved Rick and Rick loved me.

There it was. An indisputable fact in the universe at that precise moment in time. We'd been together for over a year. A year and nine weeks to be precise, I marked it up on my wall each night. Four hundred and twenty-eight days. Ten thousand, two hundred and seventy-two hours, six hundred and sixteen thousand, three hundred and twenty minutes. Most of those minutes had been ordinary; some had been special; one or two had been magical.

This moment was perfect.

I sigh with satisfaction, safe in his arms, and lean my head back against his shoulder, star-gazing. A perfect night.

And then the car went past.

Slowly, cruising down the street without a care in the world (of course not, cars don't have feelings, do they?), it passes us then comes to a halt, allowing another vehicle the right of way. I notice it because suddenly Rick says, 'What the hell?' and I look up at him and he's staring at it. Then I recognize it too, that funny little tin-can shape with its little fins and wide windscreen. It's the Triumph, his beloved Triumph Herald, and if I had any doubt at all it's soon dispelled as Rick thrusts me away from him and yells, 'OI! I WANT A WORD WITH YOU!'

He belts over to the car and yanks at the passenger door but it's locked. I can't see the driver but I know he doesn't approve because he starts revving the engine. Rick is shouting and bawling and banging on the roof and the air is blue and now people are stopping and staring, they want to know what's going on. I run up to help Rick, to force that guy out of the car, but before I get there he puts his foot down and he's away. Rick swears in frustration, picks up a stone and hurls it after the car but it's too late.

And then, before I can stop him, before I even register what he's about to do, he pulls his keys out of his pocket and he's diving into the Chevvie. And I'm yelling, 'No, Rick, you can't!' but he's not listening, he's backing out of the front garden as fast as he can. He's swerving all over the place and I'm screaming, 'No, Rick, you've been

29

'Are you all right, love?'

'She's not hurt, is she?'

'I don't think so. She's just upset.'

'Lovers' tiff.'

'Come on, get up, there's a good girl. It's cold down there.'

'Give us a hand with her, Fred.'

'I'm fine. I'm fine thanks. I'll be all right.' I stumble as they haul me to my feet.

'Don't upset yourself, love, they're not worth it.'

'I know. I'm all right.'

'D'you want us to call you a taxi? Ring for a taxi, Fred.'

'I'm fine . . . thanks . . . I can make my own way home.'

'Are you sure? Fred'll go with you. He'll see you home.'

'NO! . . . I'm fine, honest. Thank you.'

I scrub my face with my sleeve and back away from their kind, curious faces, grateful I'm in the sort of neighbourhood where people are used to this sort of stuff, where they offer practical help rather than call the police. I pull out my phone and ring Rick but there's no reply. What did I expect?

I keep ringing him all the way home. I don't know what else to do. My head's all over the place. One minute I'm expecting him to come flying round the corner, the next my mind's in overdrive, imagining terrible things. *He's got into a fight, he's driven over a bridge, he's been arrested and is in the back of a police car.* I don't even notice where I'm going but somehow, instinctively, I make my way home.

And when I see that he's not there waiting for me, I start shaking.

The house is in darkness.

I try Rick once more. Nothing.

I let myself in, what else can I do?

I tiptoe upstairs trying not to disturb anyone but Scarlett's door is ajar and, as I go past, a sleepy voice says, 'Indie, is that you?'

'Yeah.'

'Did you have a nice time?'

I try to answer but I can't. Just a broken sob.

Her door opens wide and Scarlett is there in her pyjamas, looking concerned. 'What's wrong?'

The tears roll down my face and she grabs my wrist and pulls me into her room. 'What's happened?'

I break down and tell her and she puts her arms round me and pats my back and tells me it's all right, everything will be all right, but I don't believe her.

Scarlett is as good as gold. She sits with me as I try to get hold of Rick and keeps me sane when I can't. Then, at long last, the phone is answered.

'Rick!' I gasp. 'Where are you?'

Silence. Then a woman's voice says uncertainly, 'He's not here.'

My turn to be silent. 'Who is that?' I ask eventually, my heart in my mouth.

'His mother,' she says and I relax momentarily. He must have left his phone at home.

In the background I hear a voice, slurred, gruff. 'Brenda, who the hell is that, this time of night?'

'Someone for our Rick,' she yells back.

'Tell 'em to sod off.'

She hesitates. 'Is anything wrong?'

'Brenda! I'm not telling you again!'

'No. Nothing,' I say hurriedly. 'I just wanted to speak to him that's all.'

'Is that Indie?' Her voice sounds flat and tired, but kind. 'He talks about you all the time . . .'

'Here! Give me that bloody phone!'

The phone goes dead. No help from that quarter. I turn back to Scarlett.

'Where is he?' I say helplessly. 'What could've happened to him?'

'He'll be fine,' she says, comfortingly, putting her arm round me. 'If Rick fell headfirst into the proverbial heap of s-h-i-t, he'd come up smelling of roses.'

'Scarlett, he's not fine!' I explode, shaking her off. 'He's chasing round after some nutter who's pinched his car, he's driving like a maniac *and* he's over the limit! What's *fine* about that?'

'You know Rick. He'll have given up by now. He'll have pulled in by the side of the road and be sleeping it off.'

'You reckon?' I want to believe her, I really do, but I'm scared. 'What if something's happened? Maybe we should ring the police.'

'Oh, yeah, he'd really thank you for that, wouldn't he?' She looks at me as if I've taken leave of my senses. 'Excuse me officer, I want to report that my boyfriend is driving round at night in an uninsured car wanting to kill someone. Oh, and by the way, he's been drinking. Can you find him for me and send him home please.'

I groan out loud. 'What am I going to do then?'

'Sleep on it! Like he is. Trust me, Indie, everything will be fine in the morning.'

I can tell she's dying to get back into bed by the way she keeps yawning and rubbing her eyes, even though she insists she doesn't, so eventually I go up to my room. I flop on to my bed fully-clothed, too tired to get undressed. But I can't sleep, I'm worried sick . . .

In the end I must have dropped off through sheer exhaustion because I come to suddenly. A grey light is filtering through the curtains and someone is sitting on the end of my bed. It's Scarlett. She looks worried.

I struggle to sit up. 'What is it?'

'Indie,' she says, patting me gently. 'I want you to be really brave. I'm not sure, but I think I've found him.'

30

Rick was in hospital.

Scarlett had woken up early with a clear head in the cold light of day while I was still lost in the throes of muddled sleep and had started ringing round the hospitals. She is so resourceful.

'It sounds like it could be him at the General,' she says. 'A boy was brought in last night, fair hair, about nineteen or twenty. He'd been in a car-crash. They don't know his name.'

'Oh God, it's him,' I say and I feel like I'm going to faint. 'Is he OK? Tell me he's not dead, Scarlett. He's not dead, is he?'

'No, he's not dead.'

'He must be unconscious. Otherwise they'd know who he was. Oh Scarlett!' I can feel the panic rising, choking me. I can't breathe. 'I must ring his mum and dad.' I dive for my phone but Scarlett grabs it first.

'No! Let's check out first it is him. You don't want to go upsetting them for nothing.'

She's right. She's always right. 'What should we do then?' I ask, helpless as a baby.

'Go to the hospital, of course. Make sure it's him. Come on!'

I don't wash or change or anything, we just run downstairs and race up the road as fast as we can.

One bus ride later and we're running into the main reception of the General. Even at this early hour, loads of people are milling about.

'Where do we go?' I say desperately, trying to read the proliferation of signs everywhere.

'Accident and Emergency, I guess,' says Scarlett. 'You go and sit down over there, I'll find out.'

I do as I'm told as she strides up to the main desk. I am so scared, so befuddled I just sit there, with my head in my hands, leaving it all to her. I don't know what I'd have done without her.

'They've taken him from Accident and Emergency to St Andrew's Ward.' She's back, her hand resting lightly on my shoulder. 'Come on, this way.'

She leads me by the hand through mile after mile of

corridors and eventually we come to the ward. It's quieter here away from the busy main drag and there is no sign of a member of staff.

'Should we find someone?' I whisper, but Scarlett says, 'No. We'll find him ourselves.'

He's in a side room near the entrance, on his own. His eyes are closed and he's attached to a drip. There's a whacking great bruise on his forehead and he doesn't look like Rick, he looks small and helpless. I come to a complete standstill but Scarlett opens the door and pushes me inside. I don't know what to do.

'Rick,' I whisper and to my surprise, his eyes shoot open and he looks like Rick again.

'Indie! What are you doing here?'

I fling myself at him, burying my face in his chest, but he groans and I jump back.

'Are you OK?'

'Yeah. Couple of broken ribs, bit of whiplash and concussion, but I'll live.'

'Thank God!' I reach out automatically to hug him again but he holds up his hands to ward me off. 'What happened?' I ask.

'Not sure. I can't remember. I think I must have driven into the back of him.'

'Who?'

'The guy I was chasing.'

'Was he hurt?'

'Dunno. He must've got away.'

'Have the police been involved?' asks Scarlett quietly.

Rick pulls a face. 'They were here last night but I was out of it. They're coming back later apparently. I thought you were them.'

'Don't tell them a thing,' says Scarlett immediately. I stare at her in surprise.

'It wasn't his fault!'

'No, but he shouldn't have been driving, should he? He's lost his licence, remember? Plus he'd been drinking. And driving without insurance. You don't want any more trouble, Rick. You're in enough shit as it is.'

'She's right,' moans Rick. 'But what can I do?'

'Do they know your name?'

Pause. 'Don't think so.'

'Got any ID on you? Phone, cards, driving licence?'

'No, nothing.'

'That's all right then. Make out you've lost your memory.'

'What good will that do?' I say.

'It'll give us time,' says Scarlett seriously. 'Till we've worked out what to do next.'

We leave not much longer after that, promising we'll

be back later. I don't want to abandon him there but Scarlett says we have to.

'I've just spotted a nurse on the ward. We need to scarper before she sees us. Don't want any awkward questions, do we?'

Scarlett is brilliant. She takes care of everything. She sends me home, saying, 'You'll be no good to anyone if you don't get some rest,' and sets off for college to make excuses on my behalf. I don't think I'll be able to sleep ever again but as soon as my head hits the pillow I crash out.

I dream of Rick. He's on a race track in a red car and he's chasing round and round after a white one, faster and faster, until he's spinning out of control. And now the room is spinning too and everything's whirling and swirling, twisting and turning, and I'm feeling dizzy, I feel sick, there's a ringing in my ears . . .

I wake up. My phone is ringing. It's Scarlett.

'What time is it?'

'Two.'

I've slept for hours. I scramble up in a panic. 'Rick! I need to see Rick. He's all on his own. He'll be—'

'. . . Fine. Don't worry. He's being taken care of. We'll go and see him. Meet you at the hospital in an hour. And stop freaking out. There's nothing to worry about.'

I rinse my face in cold water and catch sight of my reflection in the mirror. I hardly recognize myself. My face is pale and haunted-looking, my hair is bedraggled and there are dark shadows under my eyes. I look like Scarlett did when I first knew her.

I mean Suzie. Pathetic little Suzie Grey. Remember her?

Thank God Scarlett has taken over.

Scarlett was in charge now.

31

When I got to the hospital Scarlett was already there, sitting by Rick's bedside, holding his hand like Florence Flaming Nightingale. I felt anger surge through me like a flash of lightning, an almost welcome relief from the worry that blocked up my veins in solid, turgid lumps. What was she doing? He was my boyfriend, not hers.

I stood out of the way as a middle-aged nurse bustled around him, taking his temperature, checking the drip, tucking in sheets.

'Nice to be popular, Gary,' she remarks breezily as she moves to the end of the bed to update his notes. 'One visitor after another this afternoon. I'll leave you to it. Now, don't tire him out, girls, he needs plenty of rest.'

'Gary?' I ask, once she's disappeared.

Scarlett gets to her feet and passes me the notes. 'Indigo

Moore – meet Gary Mason.'

'Who?'

'Couldn't let them know his real name, could we? The police will be here soon.'

'But – they'll find out. They can run checks . . .'

'We'll be gone by then.'

'Gone? What are you talking about?' My eyes move from Scarlett to Rick. He seems worse than before. He doesn't just look sick now. He looks desperate.

'I've had a visitor,' he says.

'Who?'

'The guy who was in the Triumph. My Triumph. The one I crashed into.'

'Scott? What did he want?'

'Well, he didn't come to apologize, that's for sure,' says Scarlett. I dart her a look then turn my attention back to Rick.

'He said he'd come to see how I was. Acted all concerned at first. Said he had whiplash too. He asked me for my details so we could claim off our insurance.'

'But you haven't got insurance! You haven't even got a licence!'

'Exactly! I told him I didn't want to claim. I was prepared to let it go if he was. He said no, he couldn't do that, he was off work. Started to get a bit shirty. Said it was all my fault, I crashed into him. I was driving like a madman.'

''Course you were! His cheque had bounced. That's why you were chasing him!'

'I told him that. I said I was just trying to get my car back, that's all. I'd made a mistake, I shouldn't have sold it to him in the first place, it was on a finance plan.'

'What did he say?'

'Tough shit, or words to that effect.' His face is pale and he looks young, scared, vulnerable. 'He started to get nasty then. He's a shit, Ind. He wasn't having any of it.'

'Tell the police,' I say emphatically. 'Let them sort it out.'

'That's what I said. I told him I was going to report him. He laughed in my face. "What for?" he said. "Trying to get back a car you'd sold illegally? It's bleeding obvious you were driving without insurance. Bet you haven't even got a licence?" He knew, Ind. He's not stupid. Then he said, "Plus you were driving a stolen car."'

'What? You mean . . .'

'The Chevvie. It wasn't his. It was stolen. He denied completely he'd sold it to me. "Your word against mine," he said. "Where's your proof?" Clever bastard.'

'No way!'

'He's got me, Indie. Listen! I've sold a car that wasn't

245

mine to sell. And then I'm caught driving a stolen car. I've been had, Indie. I'm screwed, all ways up.' He sounds like he's about to cry.

'He's not going to get away with this!' I burst out angrily. 'I won't let him. I'll tell the police what happened. I'll tell them everything!'

'Don't be stupid,' Scarlett intervenes. 'They'll have Rick for nicking cars, selling them on, dangerous driving, driving without insurance, driving without a licence – and anything else they can throw at him. It's a prison sentence he'll be looking at, this time!' Her voice is bitter. 'I'm telling you, you'll never win against guys like him.'

'How do you know?'

'Because I know what they're like, that's why. I could write a book about them. You innocents haven't a bloody clue, in your safe little worlds.'

A shiver goes through me. My world doesn't feel very safe any more.

Rick nods sadly, wincing as the pain gets to him. 'Wish we could've worked that out before I handed over my car to him. He seemed like a nice guy in the pub.'

Scarlett snorts. 'They always do – till you get on the wrong side of them. He was very convincing. He took me in and all – and I've been round the block a bit.'

'I still think we should tell someone . . .'

Scarlett looks at me pityingly. 'Indie, listen to me. You have got to keep this to yourself. Guys like this are dangerous. It's not a game he's playing, it's serious. If he finds out you've been blabbing to the police or anyone else for that matter, he'll break your legs as soon as look at you. Or worse.'

Suddenly I'm not angry any more. I'm terrified. I stare at Scarlett helplessly, reaching out instinctively towards her for guidance. She's the only one who can help us. She knows what makes people like this tick.

'So,' I say, 'what happens now?'

'Simple,' she says. 'We disappear. We get Gary Mason out of here fast. Before the police come asking questions and Scott the Gorilla comes knuckling his way back in.'

32

So we jump Rick from hospital. I can't believe what we're doing, it's like something off a TV drama. Scarlett takes charge. She's done this before I remember, escaping from her violent boyfriend by doing a bunk from hospital. I find his clothes in the cupboard next to his bed and he tugs the drip out of his arm and gets dressed, while Scarlett keeps a look-out. When she gives the signal we nip out while the nurses are busy on the main ward. Easy-peasy, but my heart's thudding so hard it feels like it might break through my chest.

Outside the main entrance a bus is moving off, but Scarlett flags it down.

'You don't know where it's going!' I point out, but she turns back to me, a gleam in her eye.

'Who cares? Let's just get away from this place before

they get the helicopters out.'

Unbelievably, I hear myself breaking into a chuckle. Stick with Scarlett and we'll be fine. She almost sounds as if she's enjoying herself. She makes me brave too.

Luckily the bus is heading for the town centre. As it pulls into the bus station, Scarlett turns round to us and says, 'You live somewhere round here, don't you, Rick? Take him home, Indie. I'll cover for you at the salon.'

The salon? I'd totally forgotten I was due there. She thinks of everything. Momentarily I hesitate, loath to let Gordon down again and, to be honest, to relinquish more of my precious hours to her. But then she says tenderly, 'Poor Rick, you look beat. Indie will look after you,' and I feel ashamed. His face is grey with exhaustion and he's clutching his ribs. When he gets to his feet I can see he's unable to stand up straight. Get your priorities right, Indie girl, I tell myself sternly and, with his arm over my shoulder, I help him off the bus.

What a difference a day makes. Not even a day, not as much as that I think as we shuffle our way painfully down Bradford Road. Last night on this very street we were so happy, we were on top of the world. Look at us now. It was all that Scott's fault.

Rick turns the key in the lock and before he's even over the threshold the trouble begins.

'Where the hell have you been?' a man's voice yells. 'Your mother's been worried sick.'

'Stayed over at a friend's.'

'Why didn't you let us know?' A woman's voice now, thin, peeved. 'We thought something had happened to you.'

'Left my phone here.'

'Look at the state of you!' The man's voice rises even more in anger. 'Have you been fighting?'

Rick turns back to me. 'Go.'

'No! I don't want to leave you like this!'

'It's better if you do. Go on. I'll ring you later.'

He steps inside and someone, his knob of a father presumably, slams the door in my face. I turn away. Poor Rick. What am I supposed to do now?

I'm halfway home when it dawns on me that I might as well go into work after all. With a bit of luck I could still get there in time.

After all, you need all the money you can get, says a logical little voice inside my head. *You've got your sister's money to put back before she discovers it's missing.*

I debate ringing Gordon to tell him I'm on my way but I know that Scarlett will be there by now, smoothing over troubled waters for me. Don't want to complicate things.

Instead I run through the town centre as fast as I can and arrive at Herr Cutz only ten minutes late.

I charge through the door, trying to catch my breath.

'I'm here!' I call breezily, not that I'm feeling breezy, I'm worried sick, but first rule of hairdressing they teach you at college, happy and smiley at all times. 'Sorry I'm late, Gordon.'

Gordon is cutting someone's hair. He raises his head and looks at me oddly, like he's seeing me for the first time. Automatically my hand moves to my hair and I tuck a strand behind my ear and then tug my top down nervously, aware I've been wearing it for two days and nights. What must I look like? Next to him, Scarlett, looking remarkably well-groomed, is giving *my* client a comb-through. She glances up and smiles at me.

I hang up my coat and then stand there at a loss, watching them both work. He's silent, ignoring me, she's chatty and smiling. You can tell the client likes her. After a while I go over and wait beside Gordon. Finally he seems aware of my presence.

'Yes?'

'What do you want me to do?' I ask hesitantly.

'Your job,' he says crisply. Then he adds, 'Use your initiative, Indigo. I'm busy.'

I turn away, my face stinging like he's actually slapped

it. Why would he talk to me like that? I start frantically tidying up, trying to keep busy, and am relieved when the next customer walks in, a lady whose hair I've been doing for a while now. I take her coat and show her to a seat.

'Scarlett will be with you in a minute, Mrs Ward,' says Gordon and my mouth drops open.

'I can see to Mrs Ward,' I say.

'That won't be necessary, Scarlett's nearly finished.'

'But . . . !'

'Excuse me,' says Gordon to his client and takes me by the arm and marches me over to the desk. Then he says to me in a low voice bordering on venomous, a voice I don't recognize, his face centimetres from mine, 'Listen to me. Who the hell do you think you are?'

'What?'

'You waltz in when you feel like, you tell lies—'

'What lies?'

He ignores me and continues. '. . . Your mind's not on the job, quite frankly you look a mess, you can't be trusted any more—'

'I can be trusted! It's not my fault—'

'It never is, Indigo. You're taking me for a mug. I can't run a business like this. Now take twenty quid from the till and go. I don't need you.'

I stand there in shock as he goes back to his client and

continues as if nothing's happened. I want to tell him to stuff his money but I can't. I need it to pay Tamsyn back before she finds out I've nicked it. So I take a twenty-pound note from the till.

It's not going to be enough though, is it?

What the hell have I got to lose? My fingers slide back into the till and slip another four notes out from the same section. Then I slam the till shut, grab my coat and leave the salon without another word.

I can't remember the journey home, but I must've made it because the next thing I know, I'm on the doorstep searching for my key when the front door opens. Tamsyn is standing there, hands on her hips and a face like thunder.

'Where is she?'

'Who?'

'The scheming little bitch you brought into this house.'

'Scarlett? What do you want her for?'

'I want my money back.'

I swallow hard as I step round her into the house.

'What money?'

'The money she stole from my handbag.'

'Now you don't know that,' soothes my mother. 'Stop ranting and raving and come and sit down. You're just jumping to conclusions.'

I follow them into the lounge, my head in a whirl, and perch on the arm of the sofa next to Mum. Tamsyn flings herself down in an armchair and glares at me.

'Why do you think it was her?' I ask lamely.

'Duh! Because that bag's been hanging round here for days, so the alternatives are you, Mum or Dad. I don't think so!' Tam's unconditional trust in me makes me want to cry.

'You'd been out shopping that day,' points out Mum gently. 'Maybe you spent more than you thought you had?'

'Mum.' Tamsyn fixes her with an icy glare. 'I spent a fortune. But I still had a hundred quid left in my wallet.'

Tams is like me. She's good with money. She'd know exactly how much she had on her.

'Perhaps someone nicked it while you were out? A pickpocket.'

She looks at me pityingly. 'A pickpocket who opens my wallet, takes out the money and carefully puts the wallet back in my bag? Yeah, right.'

'You can't accuse Scarlett,' I say flatly. 'Not without proof.'

'Oh I'll get proof,' says Tamsyn fiercely. 'Don't you worry. And then I'm going to the police.'

33

I thought Tamsyn would never go. She sits there spitting and fuming, making dire threats about what she's planning to do to our lodger when she lays hands on her, but fortunately for Scarlett (and me!) she doesn't turn up. I keep protesting Scarlett's innocence but she's not listening. If I'd been home five minutes earlier I could've replaced the money and my sister would have been none the wiser. Instead the notes are burning a hole in my pocket.

What have I done? I'm Good Girl Indigo, I've never taken a thing that doesn't belong to me in my life and now I've stolen three times in a row. First a ten-pound tip that belonged to Scarlett, next one hundred pounds from my sister and now another eighty quid from my employer. Ex-employer.

I've turned into someone I don't recognize. I've turned into a thief. And, worse than that, I'm a thief who allows her friend to take the blame for something she hasn't done.

How the hell did all this happen?

Tamsyn leaves at last and Mum gets up and pats me on the shoulder.

'Try not to worry, love. It's not your fault. You've done your best for Scarlett, we all have. But maybe it's time she moved on.'

'But Mum – she didn't do it!'

Her eyes are warm. 'That's your trouble. You always see the best in other people.'

Other people, yes. Not in me. I can only see the worst in me.

I phone Rick to see how he is but there's no answer, he must be asleep. So I take myself off to bed.

Later on I hear Scarlett come in. She stands at my door and whispers, 'Indie?' but I pretend to be fast asleep. I can't talk to her. I don't want to hear that Gordon knows I've stolen from him. I'm too ashamed.

In the morning Mum ignores her but Scarlett doesn't notice. As soon as my parents have left for work she turns to me, her face full of concern.

'Are you OK, Indie? I can't believe how horrible Gordon was to you last night!'

I shrug as if I don't care. 'He's entitled to his opinion.'

'But he's so wrong! I told him you were looking after your boyfriend who was in a spot of bother, but he didn't want to know.'

'He's a professional. He expects professional standards.'

'But to talk to you like that! Like you were a piece of shit . . .'

My eyes sting. I can't believe Gordon said what he did to me either. He'd always been so fond of me. It was like his opinion of me had totally altered. Well, he must really hate me now he's found out I've pinched his money.

'I think he's a bit stressed,' continues Scarlett. 'He's working too hard, if you ask me. He went home not long after you and left me to cash up.'

My head jerks up. '*You* cashed up last night?'

'Yeah. Put it in the safe and all.' She looks a bit smug. 'First time I've done it. Shows he trusts me.'

She wouldn't realize money was missing. She wouldn't have a clue how much they'd taken that day.

I breathe a sigh of relief. Gordon doesn't know. Yet. He wouldn't find out till the end of the week when he did his books. I could replace it before then. After all, it's too late now to give it to Tamsyn.

Then it dawns on me. *How, exactly? You don't even work there any more.*

When we make it into college that morning, Mel rushes over to us.

'Indie! Where've you been? I've been trying to get hold of you.'

'Why? What's up?'

'Frankie's on the warpath.'

Mrs Francis, head of department. A dragon who breathes fire on students who don't pull their weight, reducing them to charred embers. My heart sinks.

'You are so dead! Where were you yesterday?'

I exchange a quick look with Scarlett, who shakes her head imperceptibly, then stare blankly at Mel. 'You missed the practical!' she prompts and I groan.

'I forgot all about it.'

It's Mel's turn to stare at me. 'I can't believe you just said that.'

'I've had a lot on my mind.'

'Indie, this is serious. You've missed loads of college and she's on your case. I can't keep covering for you.'

'You don't have to,' I say bitterly. 'I've been fired.'

'What?' She looks stricken. Mel knows how much that job meant to me. 'What for?' When I don't answer she looks at Scarlett to enlighten her but Scarlett just gives an embarrassed shrug. 'Indie, what's wrong?' she asks, her face full of concern. 'Are you in trouble?'

I want to weep. I want to fling my arms round my friend and pour out everything to her. I am on the verge of total melt-down.

But Scarlett is frowning, warning me.

And now Frankie is bearing down on me.

And then my phone is ringing and it's Rick and the sound of his voice makes me back slowly away from them all so I can hear what he's saying.

Because he sounds terrible. He sounds like he's crying.

'Where are you?' I say.

And then I'm running, running, as fast as I can, to find him.

34

He's in the park across the road. I can hear Scarlett behind me, calling my name, but I don't stop. I run straight out of college, dodging the hooting traffic, and into the gardens opposite.

He's over by the lake, pacing to and fro, arms crossed over his chest like a shield, hands tucked into his armpits.

'Rick!' I fling myself into his arms, remembering too late as he recoils in pain that his ribs are broken. He feels thin, insubstantial, beneath my hands, like he's smaller, diminished. 'What's the matter?'

He's looking terrible. He's wearing the same clothes, jeans and a hoody, and he hasn't shaved. His face is white but the bruise on his forehead is livid now, purple, black and blue with streaks of yellow, and his eyes are red-rimmed with purple shadows beneath them. He sniffs and grinds them with the pads of his hands.

'It's him,' he says. 'Scott.'

'Shit! I thought we were rid of him.' Scarlett has come up panting, behind us. 'What's he done now?'

We sink down on to the grass while Rick squats awkwardly beside us.

'He's been round my house. Making threats.'

'What sort of threats?'

'Going to the police. Other stuff. You don't want to know,' he says quickly and I know, instinctively, they involve me as well.

'How does he know where you live?' I ask, puzzled.

'He came round to see the Triumph, didn't he?'

I groan. I hadn't thought of that. 'What does he want?'

'Money. What else? He says he needs a new car, he's got whiplash and he can't work.'

'Yeah, right. You've told him you've got no insurance.'

'Not his problem,' says Rick bleakly, squinting into the distance. 'He still wants compensating.'

Silence. We watch a woman running after a toddler, a dog chasing a ball, an old man on a bench, dozing in the weak winter sunshine. Life carrying on as normal. Unbelievable.

'How much?'

'Five thousand pounds.'

'Five thousand pounds!'

'Keep your voice down!' He looks back over his shoulder as if he's expecting Scott to be lurking in the bushes. He's really scared.

'What are you going to do?' asks Scarlett quietly.

'What can I do? If he goes to the police, this time I'll get banged up inside for sure.'

'With a load of thugs and perverts,' adds Scarlett, and he looks sick.

I glare at her. 'Yeah, well maybe he won't go to the police.'

'No,' she says, 'he'll just bury him in concrete instead.'

'Scarlett!'

'It's all right, I know what the score is.' Rick gives a twisted little smile, trying to be brave, but his hands are shaking. 'I've got till this afternoon to come up with the money.'

'This afternoon? Is that all?' Scarlett looks worried. 'This guy means business.'

'Pay him off, Rick,' I say desperately.

'How?' Rick's voice rises hysterically. He's losing it. He's shivering all over now like he's in shock. He's not well and this brute of a guy is sending him over the edge. 'I haven't got any money, Indie, that's the point. I'm totally skint.'

'So am I,' I whisper.

'So, what do you want me to do, rob a bank?'

'I don't know.' Tears spill from my eyes and run down my cheeks. 'I can't do this any more.'

Scarlett sighs deeply and then she holds out her hands and takes mine and Rick's in hers. 'You two are way out of your depth,' she says. 'You need some help. Leave it to me.'

On the way home Rick and I hardly say a word. Scarlett spends most of the time on her phone talking to someone called Logan, but I can't make out what she's saying. When we get to my house we go upstairs to my room and she says, 'Right then. Put it straight on the line. How much can you two lay your hands on?'

I open my top drawer and take out the notes I'd stolen from the salon.

'Where did you get that from?' says Scarlett curiously. 'I thought you were skint.'

My answer is to shake the contents of my purse on to the bed. Rick pulls out his wallet and empties his pockets. Together the sum total comes to less than two hundred pounds.

'That's it? Nothing more hanging about anywhere? Back of a drawer? Down the side of the sofa?'

'That's it,' I say as Rick shakes his head. Scarlett blows

out her cheeks and pulls a face. Then she disappears down the stairs to her room, coming back with a handful of notes which she throws on to the bed with the rest of the money.

'That's my contribution.'

'No, Scarlett, we can't take your money . . .'

''Course you can,' she says. 'You've been good to me.'

'Thanks,' says Rick. 'I don't deserve this.'

'No,' she says, studying him, 'you probably don't.' Then she shrugs. 'You still haven't got enough though. There's not much more than three hundred quid here.'

'D'you think you can stall him?' I ask Rick. 'Give him this to be going on with and tell him you'll get the rest as soon as you can?'

He shakes his head again, more emphatically this time. 'No way. You haven't met him, have you?'

'This guy sounds like he's not going to be messed around. You need to give him all the money in one go to get rid of him.' Scarlett hesitates as if she's making up her mind. 'I think it's time you met Logan.'

'Who's Logan?'

'Someone I know. Someone I've had dealings with.'

In the end, it was just Scarlett and me that went to see Logan. Rick was in a bad way, off his head with pain and lack of sleep.

'Why don't you crash down here?' suggests Scarlett. 'Get some sleep. Indie and me, we can sort this out. When we come back we'll have the rest of the money for you. Then you can hand it over to Scott the Scav and be rid of him.'

Scott the Scav. Scott the Gorilla. Good old Scarlett. The way she refers to the bully who is terrorizing my boyfriend diminishes him, making him less scary, like a kid's cartoon villain. Rick doesn't take much convincing.

We'd arranged to meet Logan behind the station. 'How do you know him?' I ask Scarlett as we make our way there. There's something menacing about this area with its boarded-up shops and thin-faced people scurrying like rats from hole to hole.

'You get to know people when you're on the streets. Logan is one of the good guys. He found me a bed in that hostel on Dock Street. Lent me some money till I got straight.'

'For nothing?'

'Well no, he charged me interest, natch. Not much though. I've paid it all off now.' She looks proud of herself.

He's waiting for us, leaning back against the wall, smoking a cigarette. One of those cool-but-scary-looking guys with a hard, stubbled face, dressed in the street uniform of hoody, jeans and trainers, a beanie pulled down low under his hood.

When he sees us he unfolds himself to his full height and now I'm scared. What the hell are we getting ourselves into here? I've heard about loan sharks.

But then his face breaks into a wide grin and he says to Scarlett, 'Look at you! I hardly recognized you!' in obvious admiration and Scarlett grins back as they high-five each other. The tight little knot in my throat that had been threatening to choke me loosens at last and I'm not so scared any more.

'Done well for myself, haven't I? And it's all thanks to her. This is my friend, Indie.'

'Nice to meet you, Indie.' He studies me carefully. 'You in a spot of bother, Scarlett said.'

I hesitate, wondering where to start.

'S'all right,' he says quickly. 'I don't need to know. You wanna borrow some money, yeah?'

'Yes please.'

'How much?'

'Four thousand seven hundred pounds. And I need it by this afternoon.'

He chuckles low in his throat. 'Feisty!'

'Better round it up to five grand,' suggests Scarlett and he shrugs like it's no odds.

'Can you do it then?'

'It's possible.'

'Is it going to cost me?'

'Of course.' He looks at me steadily. 'I'm not a charity.'

I like his honesty.

'How much?'

'Ten per cent.'

'Ten per cent?' I echo.

'I can't go any lower,' he says, looking really regretful. 'Sorry.'

'That's what he charged me, Ind,' says Scarlett eagerly. 'It's a really good rate.'

They've misunderstood me. I know it's a good rate. Credit cards charge loads more than that, don't they? About twenty-six per cent.

We could manage that between us, Rick and me.

'How long do I have to repay you?'

He breathes out cigarette smoke through his nose, appraising me. 'Long as it takes,' he says finally. 'Something tells me you're the sort of girl who'll settle her debts pretty quick.'

'I am.'

'It's better than you'd get anywhere else,' he says evenly. 'Take it or leave it.'

I nod. 'I'll take it.'

270

35

We wait around for an hour or two while Logan goes off to get the money. Scarlett asks me if I want to get something to eat but I'm not hungry. Now it's nearly over I feel sick. We go into a café and she eats burger and chips but all I can manage is black coffee. She has to buy that for me because I'm broke.

Mel keeps texting me, wanting to know why I'd run off. I text her back to say I'm fine.

Logan comes back at last and hands me a brown envelope and I take it into the loo to count it out. Five grand in used notes doesn't look much, but it's all there.

'You want a receipt for this?' I ask when I come back. He shakes his head.

'No need. I trust you.'

'Thanks. Can you write down the terms for me?'

'Terms?'

'Repayments and that.'

He gives me a big wide grin and taps his head. 'It's all up here, Indie love. That's my filing system. Never forget a thing. Ten per cent we agreed on.'

I nod. Scarlett is my witness and she can vouch for him. That's the best guarantee I could have. Relief washes over me as he puts out his hand.

'It's a deal, Indie girl. Nice doing business with you.'

I shake his hand. Strong, firm, dependable. You can always tell a man's character by his handshake, my dad says.

Thank you, Scarlett, for putting me in touch with this unlikely angel. I can't believe it's all been so easy.

We go home to Rick to give him the money. He's crashed out on my bed, sleeping like a baby, and it strikes me how young and innocent he looks compared to big, tough, streetwise Logan. When I wake him and hand him the envelope his face lights up like a kid at Christmas.

'How did you do it?'

'Don't thank me, thank Scarlett.'

'Thank Logan,' she says, brushing it off.

'I don't know what to say . . .'

His voice is full of gratitude but she cuts him off impatiently.

'Just pay him off, Rick, and be done with it. You'll never win against a guy like Scott.'

She sounds like he's irritating her. I remind myself that Scarlett's been around, she's encountered practically every kind of low-life there is in her short life and she's had to fend for herself. It's hardly surprising if she's a bit short on sympathy. She more than makes up for it in practical help.

I don't know what we'd have done without her.

'What time are you meeting him?' I ask.

'Three,' says Rick. 'I'd better head off.'

'I'll come with you.'

'No, you're coming to college with me,' says Scarlett and I look at her in surprise. 'Mel's been texting me all morning to see where you are. You're in enough trouble as it is.'

I am in deep shit at college. Frankie wants to see me. She gives it to me straight, right down the line. *I've missed so many sessions, I haven't got my work in, I'm in danger of failing this module, I'll be out on my ear if I'm not careful, blah, blah, blah*. It washes over me like she's talking about someone else. I'm too exhausted to care.

'What *is* the matter with you, Indigo?' she asks in exasperation. 'You were one of the best students we'd ever had. Everyone spoke so highly of you.' She sits there and I know she's waiting for an answer.

'Things have been difficult,' I say at last, giving her what she wants. Her face alters and she switches immediately into caring mode.

'What is it, dear? Home? Friends? Boyfriend trouble? Money?' Take your pick, I think bitterly. 'I know how hard it is for you young people nowadays,' she continues, her voice soft now. 'The pressures you're all under . . .'

You haven't a clue, I think wearily. Why would you? I hadn't either till a few months ago. Until Scarlett walked into my life, I thought the world revolved around me.

My life was all mapped out. Sail through college. Nice job at Herr Cutz to look forward to afterwards. Put a bit of money by then, perhaps in a year or two, if I could stop him spending too much on those infernal cars, Rick and I could afford a place of our own. Maybe we'd even get married one day, have kids together, a boy for him and a girl for me. He'd have his own garage, I'd have my own salon.

That wasn't too much to ask for, was it? It's only what most of us want. My eyes prickle with unshed tears.

I was being greedy. Scarlett knew. People like her

didn't expect a home, family, financial security as a right. And neither should people like me. Because, let's face it, scratch the surface and there's not a lot of difference between Scarlett and me, not really. Not now everything's changed.

I assumed the world was divided into winners and losers. And I was a winner. Naturally.

My internal defence mechanism kicks in. But you were a nice winner. You always tried to help the losers. Then, from deep somewhere in my subconscious, Scarlett's words jeer back at me. '*Get off on it, do you? Makes you feel better about yourself?*'

How arrogant was I? Yeah, well now I know what it feels like. 'Cause I'm a loser too.

I bury my face in my hands.

'Don't worry, dear. We'll work something out for you. We'll get you back on track.' Frankie is on her knees beside me, pity engrained all over her carefully made-up face. 'I think you've taken too much on lately. Your friend Mel tells me you've been working at Herr Cutz in the evenings. Gordon Smith is a very nice man and he's always spoken most highly of you. Let me give him a ring and see if we can sort this out.'

'No!' My panic is such that I actually grab her arm as she reaches for the phone. 'You're right. I've already sorted it. I'm not working there any more. Except for my placement, that is,' I add hurriedly as her face registers surprise, though I don't even know if that's true any more. 'I'll catch up with my work, I promise.'

'Good.' She pats my hands with relief and struggles to her feet. 'I want to see you completely back on track by the end of term. You're a sensible girl, Indigo. I know you won't let me down.'

'I won't,' I promise and I meant it.

I never intended to let anyone down. But I did.

Myself more than anyone.

'So, let me just recap here.'

Her voice in the darkness, soft but intrusive.

'You borrowed five thousand pounds from a complete stranger to give to your boyfriend.'

'He wasn't a complete stranger. Scarlett knew him.'

'To pay back this man who claimed Rick had driven into him.'

'Claimed, nothing. Rick did drive into him.' I feel myself getting cross. What does she know about it? 'He smashed up his car.'

'Did you see it?'

'What?'

'The car. Did you see it after Rick had driven into it?'

'No. But it was a total write-off apparently.'

'Did Rick see it?'

'No . . .'

'Why not?'

'Well, Rick was out of it. And then . . . I guess the police took both cars away.'

Silence.

'But the guy, Scott, he was badly injured. He couldn't go to

277

work any more. He had whiplash . . .'

'How do you know that?'

'He said! He told Rick . . .'

She doesn't need to say any more. But she does.

'Let me get this straight. A man called Scott bought Rick's car in a pub . . .'

'Yes.'

'. . . but the cheque bounced . . .'

'Yes.'

'. . . and he gave him another car in part-exchange . . .'

'Yes.'

'. . . which turned out to be stolen . . .'

'Yes.'

'. . . and then Rick just happens to crash into Scott's car . . .'

'Yes.'

'. . . and Scott demands five thousand pounds in compensation from Rick.'

'Yes.'

Pause.

She's not telling me. She's helping me work it all out for myself.

'Scott set us up from the start. It's obvious,' I say sadly. I knew it already deep down. But now I can see it all clearly.

'And then you borrowed five grand from a moneylender to make him go away?'

'Yes! It was the only thing I could do. Rick would've ended up in prison otherwise. Or worse.'

'And did he?' she asks gently. 'Did Scott go away?'

The tears start flowing again. 'No, of course he didn't.'

36

When Rick called me to say he'd paid Scott off, I genuinely thought the nightmare was over.

Don't get me wrong, I knew we still had a massive debt to Logan. And I didn't have a job any more. Plus there was a small matter of the money I'd stolen from my sister and the salon to sort out. And Rick still had to pay off the finance company. We weren't out of the woods by a long way.

But my overriding feeling was one of relief that we would be rid once and for all of Scott, a man I'd never even set eyes on but whose presence in our lives threatened me more than I would ever be prepared to admit.

How wrong could you be?

My alarm goes off at seven a.m. I'd set it the night before

so I could make an early start. A fresh start.

Today I was going to spend the whole day in college, working my socks off to save my flagging college career. And afterwards I would go to the salon, cap in hand, explain to Gordon what had been going on and try, goodness knows how, to slip the money back before he'd noticed it had gone missing. I'd made up my mind.

'You're looking better today,' remarks Scarlett as we make our way to college. Mum had ignored her again this morning but she still didn't seem to notice. Last night Mum had asked me once more when she was planning to move on. I'd said I'd have a word with her but now didn't seem the time.

'All thanks to you and Logan,' I say. 'I feel like a huge weight has lifted from my shoulders.'

'Glad to be of help,' she says, like it's no big deal. But it is. My boyfriend could have been in jail or beaten up or worse if she hadn't come to the rescue. Weird to think how it was me who'd rescued her in the first place not that many months ago. Who would've thought our fortunes could have changed so drastically in such a short space of time? In a way I would be glad when she did move on because Scarlett, through no fault of her own, seemed to have brought a whole heap of bad luck with her when she moved into my life.

But then she tucks her arm through mine and says, 'That's what friends are for,' and I'm overwhelmed with gratitude.

The day is good. I put everything firmly out of my mind and buckle down to work, attending all my lectures and catching up in the library in between.

Frankie pops her head in during a practical session and beams at me. 'Everything going well, dear?' she trills in her budgie voice and disappears without waiting for an answer. It's blatantly obvious she's checking up on me. Beside me Mel giggles and I laugh too for the first time in days.

'You OK now?' she asks.

'Not bad.'

'Do you want to talk about it?'

'Yeah. But not now.'

'After college?'

I shake my head ruefully. 'There's something I've got to do. I need to go into work. But soon . . .'

'OK.' She smiles at me understandingly. 'I'm not going anywhere.'

I smile back, wondering why I hadn't confided in Mel more. Because it was Rick's problem I guess and had to be kept secret.

And because Scarlett was always there for me.

* * *

I'd seen Rick briefly at lunchtime. Like me he was glad it was over and he was revelling being back in the routine of the workshop. He told everyone he'd written off his car and didn't want to talk about it and after a bit of leg-pulling from his mates, they'd let it go.

Then, as I'm leaving college, I see him again. He's running over to me from the direction of the workshops, his face screwed up. His ribs must be hurting. Then as he gets closer I see it's more than that, something has happened, and my stomach plummets. He stops next to me, holding his side and gasping for breath.

'He's back.'

'Who?' I say automatically, but I know exactly who he means.

'He wants more money. It's not enough. His car's in a worse state than he thought.'

'Bloody hell, Rick!'

'I know!' His eyes are wild, like an animal that's been cornered, and he's sweating. I can practically smell his fear. Irrationally I am angry with him. I want him to take charge, to deal with it himself. I don't want to be part of this any more, it's nothing to do with me.

I want my tall, good-looking, sweet-natured guy to be someone else. Someone tougher, harder, someone

284

who can take care of himself, someone who doesn't have to come running to me every time something goes wrong.

Someone like Logan.

'How much?'

'Another grand.'

'Where are you supposed to get that from?'

He says nothing. He doesn't have to. It's obvious. *He's* not supposed to get it from anywhere. I am.

So I went back to Logan.

Scarlett sets it up and insists on coming with me. We meet him in a disused shop doorway in Back Street, a street that looks like it sounds. To my surprise straightaway he pulls an envelope out of his inside pocket and hands it to me. Why does someone walk round with that amount of money on him? Not for the first time I wonder how he makes it. Is he a drug-dealer? My stomach knots with fear and suddenly I find myself shaking my head and pushing it back at him.

'I can't take it.'

'Why not?' He looks at Scarlett and for the first time I see a flash of anger, like he thinks we're wasting his time. 'I thought you said she wanted another grand.'

'She does. Don't mess about, Indie.'

'I can't. It's too much. I won't be able to pay it back.' I'm panicking. I don't understand this world. I don't know what I'm getting myself into.

"Course you will,' he says soothingly and now his eyes are warm with sympathy. 'You've got yourself tangled up with this low-life and you're scared, that's understandable. But believe me, you're far better owing me this money than him. I know how these guys operate.'

'He's right, Indie,' says Scarlett and I turn to her in anguish.

'But what if he wants more? What do I do then?'

'Don't worry,' says Logan crisply. 'If he wants more than that, he's getting greedy. We've got ways of dealing with people like him. That'll be another ten per cent by the way.'

We? It sounds like Logan's got a whole network of people working with him. I'd assumed he was on his own.

What did I know? Like Alice, I'd fallen through a hole, but instead of finding myself in Wonderland I was trapped in a scary underworld with no way out. What choice did I have?

He was right about one thing though. I'd rather owe him money than someone like Scott.

I took the grand.

37

We were never going to win against Scott. I knew that as soon as he turned up for the third time, wanting more money from Rick.

'Tell him to get stuffed,' I said, so Rick did, even though he was bricking it.

Soon after, the phone calls started.

'How did he get my number?' Rick says, hollow-eyed. They'd continued all night long.

'I don't know.' I'm as bewildered as he is.

'I'm never going to get rid of him, Indie. He knows where I live, he's got my number . . .'

Rick is starting to sound desperate. He's no way as strong as I thought he was.

'He'll back off when he realizes you're not going to pay him any more,' I say with more conviction than I feel. I can't keep bailing Rick out.

'Indie, you don't know what he's threatening to do!'

'Tell me then!'

He shakes his head and I'm absolutely certain it's something to do with me. But all he says is, 'I don't think he's acting alone. I think there's a gang of them,' and my heart sinks even further.

That night when I'm in my room in a vain attempt at studying, there's a knock at my door. It's Scarlett and she looks upset.

'What's wrong?'

'Well, it might be nothing but . . .'

'What?'

'I was coming home from work tonight, right?'

'Right,' I say sourly. For all my good intentions I still hadn't made it back to the salon to sort things out with Gordon and I didn't know if I ever would. There was too much going on here.

'And I'm pretty sure someone was following me.'

My heart beats hard against my chest. 'Who?'

'Dunno. He was in a car.'

'Like a kerb-crawler you mean?'

'Yeah, I guess so. All the way home, right to the front door. He just kept tailing me.'

'What did he say?'

'Nothing. I couldn't even see who it was. The windows were blacked out.' She shivers. 'There may have been more than one person in it.'

I stare at her. It must've been pretty scary to unsettle tough little Scarlett. Suddenly she strides over to the velux window and pulls it wide open and I scramble up next to her and put my head out to peer down into the street below. Cars are lined up all along the road. As we watch, one pulls away from the kerb.

'Is that it?'

'I dunno, I can't tell from up here.' She looks shaken. I slam the window shut.

Then my phone rings and it's Rick. He's in a state. I listen to him unload and then when he's done I throw my phone across the room and hold my head in my hands.

'Indie?'

I look up, my eyes brimming. Scarlett's face is full of concern.

'Scott wants one more grand, and that'll be the end of it. Otherwise things will turn really nasty. Oh, and by the way, he says, "Nice house your girlfriends live in". He knows where I am, Scarlett. And you. He could get us anytime.'

She groans.

'D'you think he means it?'

'Oh yeah, he means it, all right.' She sits there looking scared, biting her nails. 'D'you know what?' she says in the end. 'I think we should go back to see Logan.'

So we do. Just Scarlett and me. I ring Rick back and tell him this is definitely the last time. He offers to come with us but Scarlett says Logan might not like it, she'd have to ask him first. So I say, let's just go, because I want to get this whole business over and done with. And, to be honest, I don't think Rick would be a lot of help.

Logan has the grand all ready for me in an envelope. Just as I'm about to take it, it hits me.

This will mean you're seven thousand pounds in debt to this man and you haven't a clue how you're supposed to pay it back.

I shake my head in despair. 'It's no good. I can't.'

'Why not?' That hint of impatience again. 'Here. Take it.'

'No. I give up. I'm going to the police. I'm going to tell them everything.'

'Like what?'

'That Scott's been blackmailing us. That I've already given him six thousand pounds and he still wants more.'

'You sure that's a good idea? Ain't that going to get your pretty boyfriend into a whole lot of trouble?'

'He's already in a whole lot of trouble . . .'

'They're going to wanna know where you got the money from.'

'I'll tell them – I borrowed it from you.'

He shakes his head from side to side, his face expressionless. 'Uh-uh. I don't think that's a good idea, Indie girl.'

Scarlett looks at me anxiously. 'Logan won't want the police poking their noses into his business, Indie.'

No of course he won't.

'Take it,' says Logan, holding the envelope out to me. 'You need to pay him off once and for all, that's the important thing. You don't want anything happening to that boyfriend of yours. Or worse still to you or little Scarlett here.'

'But I don't know how I can pay it back!' I howl. 'I've no money, no job . . .'

'Don't worry! That's my problem. Am I hassling you for it? No little sister, you've got enough on your plate already.' His eyes are warm and smiling now. 'Hey, Red Riding Hood, who d'you think I am? The Big Bad Wolf? You think I'm going to eat you up?'

No, not you. That's Scott. I'd wandered into a fairytale

and discovered it was a horror story. But lucky for me, Logan was in the story too with a big axe in his hands ready to cut Scott right back down to size.

My hand comes out to take the money.

'OK. Thanks. But this is the last time, I promise.'

I don't know what Rick said to him, but he must've made it clear there'd be no more money forthcoming because Scott went quiet. Rick was jubilant, he thought it was all over, but I was more cautious, we'd been there before. Plus, despite Logan's comforting words, I was tying myself in knots about the repayments. At the end of the day I owed him seven grand with no means of repaying it.

And though Rick said different, the fact remained it was my debt, not his.

'I think it's time Scarlett found herself somewhere to live,' Mum announces one day when Scarlett's at work. 'It was only ever going to be temporary.'

Yeah, temporary till my sister made the incorrect assumption she was a tea-leaf and wanted her out of the house. My cheeks burn at the memory.

'She's got nowhere to go. You can't chuck her out on the streets.'

'Don't be silly. She's not destitute any more. She's got

friends now, a job. She can stand on her own two feet.'

She was right. I was the penniless one, not Scarlett. But the fact remained, I still had a home. She didn't. And Scarlett had been good to me. How could I ask her to go after all she'd done for me?

'Christmas is coming, Mum,' I say. 'Have a heart.'

Now Mum's cheeks turn pink. She's one of the kindest people I know. 'I do have a heart, Indigo. And my heart tells me that if it's a straight choice between having Scarlett here for Christmas or Tamsyn, then your sister wins every time. And she will not set foot in this house as long as that girl is here.'

'But . . .'

Was I about to blurt out the truth and open a whole can of worms? Was I going to say you're all wrong, it wasn't Scarlett who nicked Tam's money, it was me? Your precious daughter's turned into a thief. And if I had, would she have helped me to sort out the whole stinking mess I'd somehow got myself into?

I'll never know because she cut me off before I could I say another word.

'But nothing! My mind's made up, Indigo, and we all think the same. That girl has abused her hospitality and outstayed her welcome and I don't trust her any more. It's time for her to go. And if you won't tell her, I will!'

38

I make up my mind to have a word with Scarlett the next day. But first I talk to Mel about it.

'My mum wants her out.'

'I don't blame her.'

'I thought you liked her now?'

'She's all right. Better than I thought. But I wouldn't want her living with me permanently.'

'Oh. I was going to ask if she could move in with you.'

'Are you serious?' She looks horrified and I laugh for the first time in ages.

'I feel responsible for her,' I admit. 'She hasn't got anyone else.'

'She's got a boyfriend.'

'Has she?' I stare at her in surprise. Then I remember I'd wondered that myself, though the events of the last few weeks had sent everything else out of my head.

'Chloe's said she's seen her with someone. Big guy, not bad-looking.'

The penny drops. 'That's Logan. He's just someone she knows.'

She shrugs. 'Chloe didn't give that impression. Anyway, you don't owe her a thing. You've been good to her.'

'She's been good to me.'

Mel looks at me oddly. She doesn't know the huge debt I owe Scarlett for all the help she's given me sorting out Rick's mess. And now I'm about to chuck her back on the streets.

'Just tell her it's time she moved on. She's not stupid. She can work that out for herself.'

She makes it sound so simple. Maybe it is.

'Can you hang on a minute?' I say, tugging at Scarlett's arm as the café empties out after lunch. 'I want a word.'

Mel gives me a little smile as she moves off and Scarlett catches it. 'What's going on?' she asks suspiciously.

'Nothing! Sit down. I want to speak to you.'

'What about?'

I should've thought this through more. 'Christmas.'

Her face lights up. 'Yey! Can't wait. Never had a proper family Christmas before. Turkey, tree, presents . . .'

'That's just it . . .'

'Aahh. Don't worry about buying me a present, hon. I know you're skint. It's enough for me to spend it in a proper home for once. It doesn't stop me buying one for you though!'

This is going so badly. 'The thing is, Tamsyn will be home for Christmas . . .'

'Yeah?'

'. . . And she'll want her room back.'

'That's OK. I'll move upstairs with you – if that's all right.' When I don't reply her eyes narrow. 'It *is* all right, innit?'

'Well, Mum thought – I mean, *we* thought – you might be ready to move on. You know, find yourself somewhere else to live. Get a place of your own . . .'

'You want me out?'

'No! That is . . . Mum said . . . it's awkward . . . I don't know what to say . . .'

'What have I done?' Her face is fierce but at the same time bemused, like a wounded animal which lost a fight it expected to win.

'Nothing!'

'I must've done something if you're chucking me out.'

'I'm not chucking you out! I thought – *we* thought – you might want to be a bit more independent, that's all.'

'Like you, you mean?' Her face is sharp now, jeering at me. 'You'd have been in a right mess without me to look after you – and this is all the reward I get. You want to get rid of me now you think you're out of the woods.'

'I don't, Scarlett! It's not like that!'

'What is it like then?' she spits, her face vicious now. 'Thanks Scarlett, now piss off!'

She gets to her feet and I grab her hand but she shakes it off. The contempt in her face is unbearable.

'Bitch!' she rasps and stalks off. 'Who wants to be around you anyway? You're in danger, girl!'

By the time I get home she's cleared out and gone.

39

The next day Scott asks for more money. I can't believe it when Rick tells me.

'I don't know what to do,' he says.

'Change your bloody number!' I snap, and he looks at me startled. I never used to swear. I never used to steal from people either. All this stuff that's been going on has made me into a different person. Someone I don't like.

'He's coming after me,' says Rick tonelessly, and I shout, 'Stand up to him then!' even though I know that's not fair. Since the crash Rick has been a pruned-back, pared-down version of his former self.

Face the facts, Indie. Your boyfriend is weak. Maybe he always was.

Then he says, 'He's going to get you too,' and I feel sick.

'We need help!' I whisper, and he says, 'No! We're in

too deep. You can't tell anyone!' and I promise him I won't.

Because the truth is, there's no one to tell. There's no one left to turn to. Scarlett's gone and even if I knew where she was, I couldn't ask her for help. I'd let her down, why would she help me? Panic strikes as it dawns on me, too late, that with her departure from my life, Logan has disappeared too. The one person I believed capable of standing up to Scott. The one person who could get rid of the parasite that was destroying my life. The one person with whom I felt safe.

'THIS IS ALL YOUR FAULT!' I scream and then I hit Rick hard across the face. He looks back at me, his face stupid with shock, and then I lose it, totally, scratching, punching, pulling his hair, wailing all the time like a banshee. He gasps then grabs me by the wrists and I'm twisting and writhing, trying to pull away from him, but I can't escape. I kick out, spitting at him, calling him vile names, shrieking out awful stuff I never even knew I felt, and his arms come round me and he holds me tight. I try to throw him off and we stagger around in a jerking, spasmodic, zombie-like dance but he won't let me go. Gradually the dance slows down as my body is racked by deep, tearing sobs and I sink to the ground and he kneels there with me, holding me, until it is over.

* * *

Scott was never going to disappear from our lives. I know that now.

And neither was Logan. I owed him seven thousand pounds.

After that fight (can you call it a fight when it's completely one-sided?), after that crazy, frightening, shameful letting-go, I felt totally empty and washed-out like wreckage floating on the surface of the sea. I had no idea if I would ever reach the shore.

There was no sign of Scarlett. I tried her number loads of times but it always went straight to answer phone. She wasn't at college and no one had seen her. I debated going to the salon to see if she was there but I wouldn't have known what to say to her. Nor to Gordon for that matter. He had to have found out I'd nicked money from the till by now and I didn't have the strength to face him. I imagined what those two would be saying about me while they stood next to each other doing hair and I felt sad when I thought of Linda, Kay and maybe even Shazza chipping in.

I overheard Mum and Tams going on about Scarlett but I couldn't even be bothered to stand up for her. It was like someone had switched off the feeling, caring part of me. All I could think of was how long it would take for Logan to get in touch.

301

Not that long as it happened. My phone went in the middle of the night, dragging me from much-needed sleep. I was disorientated, the sound painful to my ears, like it was splitting my brain in two. For a moment I was petrified it was Scott, but it was Logan's voice who said, 'Indie?' and my heart leaped. My saviour, come to rescue me. I never even questioned where he'd got my number from. In this strange new world I was living in, people seemed to get whatever they wanted.

'Logan!'

'Hi. Haven't heard from you for a while. That guy off your case?'

'No. He keeps asking for more.'

I expect him to say he'll take care of him now, like he promised. But instead he says, 'D'you want another grand?'

'No. Definitely not. I just want to be rid of him.'

'What? You want me to bump him off?' He sounds amused. ''Cause that'll cost you a bit more.'

I giggle nervously. 'You are joking, aren't you?'

'I never joke, Indie,' he says, his voice serious, and though I'm pretty sure he's pulling my leg, his words make me shiver.

'Anyway, down to business.' His tone is light again now. 'We need to set up some repayments.'

'Repayments?'

'Yep. Now, let me see. Five grand at ten per cent is what we agreed. That'll be five hundred quid you owe me.'

'Five hundred pounds?' I repeat faintly.

'For the first loan. Then one grand at twenty per cent. That's another two hundred quid . . .'

'Twenty per cent?'

'Plus another grand at thirty per cent. That's another three hundred quid on top.'

'Thirty per cent? You said it would cost me ten per cent!'

'For the first loan, yeah. After that it goes up ten per cent each time. I told you that.'

'Did you?' I rack my brains but I can't remember.

'It's standard practice, Indie.'

'But that's . . .' I'm trying desperately to keep up with the figures, but none of it makes sense.

'A grand in total, if my maths is correct. Want me to go over it again? Don't want you to think I'm cheating you.'

My mouth feels dry as dust but I manage to say in a strangled voice, 'When d'you want it by?'

'End of the month, of course. Got to balance the books.'

'That's – Friday.'

'So it is.'

Silence. Then he adds, 'Is that a problem, Indie?'

'No!' I say wildly. 'Only, I never knew the interest would be that much.'

'You agreed.'

'Yeah, I know I did. But if I'd gone to a bank it would have been cheaper . . .'

'I'm not a bank.'

'No, I understand that. But I didn't know . . . I didn't realize . . .'

'You agreed, Indie,' he repeats evenly. 'No one forced you. You came to me.'

'I know! I just don't know how I'm going to get it . . .'

He sighs. 'That's your problem. You should've thought of that before. I'll phone you in the morning.'

He rang me first thing before I was even out of bed. To see how I was, he said. He sounded friendly and normal, his voice fresh and light, like he'd had a good night's sleep.

Not like me.

'Logan, I haven't slept a wink. I've been racking my brains all night long. I can't get the money for you by Friday. It's Friday tomorrow!'

'Why not?'

'I haven't got any! That's the point. That's why I borrowed from you in the first place.'

304

'But it wasn't a gift, Indie. You always knew you had to pay it back.'

'I know! But not so soon. I thought I'd have more time.'

'I'm not asking for the whole debt,' he says patiently, like he's talking to a child. 'I'm just asking you for one month's interest.'

One month! So I would have to find this sum every month! And I still wouldn't have paid off the seven grand.

'The thing is,' he says, like he's a mind-reader, 'if you leave it, the rates go up sky-high. You're better off keeping up with the repayments.'

'I can't!' I whisper. 'I haven't got it.'

He sighs deeply. 'Indie, I wish I could help you, but my hands are tied. I'm not a one-man band, I'm just the front man. My boss wants a thousand pounds by tomorrow, bottom line.'

I don't say anything. I can't.

'A word of warning, don't mess with him, girl.' His voice is soft, kind even, but I have never felt so threatened in my whole life.

What sort of world had I got myself into? I'd assumed Scott was acting on his own, a lone hungry wolf, only to be pursued by men in blacked-out cars. Now it turns out Logan, my saviour, my knight in shining armour, is a predator too, with a vicious boss telling him what to do.

They were all around me, circling, waiting to attack. They would tear me to pieces, the whole ravenous pack of them, and there was nothing I could do to stop it. I start to whimper.

'Hey, don't stress, Indie,' he says soothingly. 'Look, it doesn't have to be cash. A credit card will do.'

'I haven't got one,' I moan. 'I had a debit card but I was overdrawn. I had to close my account.'

'Tch-tch. Not very good with money, are you?'

He sounds amused again and I feel like screaming, 'I used to be, once – before I met Scarlett!' but I don't because none of this is her fault.

'They won't be fussy whose name is on the card,' he says casually. 'Maybe you've got access to someone else's. A family member perhaps?'

I know what he's suggesting. 'I don't know . . .' I say, stalling, as I try to get my head around it. Steal from my own family. I can't do that.

But you've done it before.

Then he starts to get impatient.

'Look, Indie, you don't have any choice. You know you can be prosecuted and sent to prison if you don't pay up. I'm trying my best to help you here. You've got till tomorrow to think about it.'

And then the phone went dead.

'I don't know what to do.'

'You're frightened,' she says softly, and I nod though she can't see me. 'What is it that frightens you?'

Where do I begin?

'I'm scared of Scott. And Logan.' The tears run down my chin. 'And I don't want to go to prison.'

'You won't,' she says, but not in a consoling way, in a matter-of-fact way, and it gets my attention.

'Why not?'

'Because you haven't committed a crime.'

'But Logan said if I don't pay up—'

'If you have borrowed money from an unlicensed moneylender you have no obligation to pay it back.'

'But Logan said—'

'Logan has no legal right to lend money. He's a loan shark—'

'How do you know that?'

'He pretends to be friendly. He's got no paperwork. He was vague about the repayment period and misled you about the interest rates. He's asking you for a bank card for access to someone else's money. He's already made threats, enough to

307

terrify you – it's pretty obvious.'

I know. I know it is now. I think I knew all along but I just wouldn't admit it to myself.

'You haven't committed a crime. He has. And it's he *who could be looking at a prison sentence, not you.'*

'How do you know all this?' I whisper.

She's quiet for a moment before she answers, her voice low and regretful. 'I'm afraid I hear stories like this all the time. You're not the first to be had, Indie, and you certainly won't be the last.'

40

As it sinks in that actually *I* am not responsible in the eyes of the law for this huge debt I've built up, all my fear, pain and tension slowly drains away, leaving me dizzy and weak with relief.

Mrs Moffat, I can never thank you enough. With your calm, straightforward analysis of the situation and your gentle, patient concern, you've made me feel I'm no longer alone.

And, knowing this, I don't need you any more. But now it's you that won't let me go until I reassure you once more that no, I have absolutely no intention of finding my way out of this crazy situation I've got myself into by taking my own life.

And then, finally, I end the phone call.

When I look at my watch I can't believe how long

we've been talking. Part of me wants to sink into oblivion, crash out for a week; the other wants to celebrate, call Rick with the good news, no, scream it from the rooftops! We're going to get our lives back at last!

But my relief is short-lived. Before long my exhausted brain goes into overdrive and the fear returns.

You see, like Mrs Moffat said, I might not be the first or the last sucker in the world to fall victim to a loan shark. But, I'm certainly one of the unluckiest. I've got myself tangled up with not one, but *two* sets of villains and, though her information has been enlightening, it doesn't allay all my fears. Because, let's face it, going to prison is probably the least of my worries, when you've got thugs like Scott and Logan breathing down your neck.

Knowledge is power. I need to know exactly what I'm up against. I jump off my bed and switch on my computer. Then I type *Loan sharks* into the search engine.

I wish I hadn't. It's horrendous. Much worse than I thought it was. Loan sharks are everywhere. There's a frenzy of them that prey on people in need, pretending to help at first and then, once they've got them in their clutches, extorting money from them by threats and actual acts of violence. Crazy money! I can't believe I've been so stupid. I trawl through heartbreaking stories.

A woman who lost everything, her home, her marriage, her kids, after she fell prey to one of these scumbags, all for a wide-screen television to watch the Olympics on. A man made redundant, desperate to keep up his mortgage repayments, beaten to a bloody pulp and left for dead in a dark alley. A terrified student who hanged himself, another forced into prostitution, a third who became a drugs mule until the illegal drugs she was carrying internally burst open and killed her. A man who had a heart attack, literally frightened to death by the weight of his debt and the ruthless, manipulative scum who preyed upon him.

No wonder Mrs Moffat made me promise not to commit suicide. Compared to this catalogue of human fear and misery, a packet of pills washed down with a bottle of vodka seems like an easy way out. Oblivion.

But you promised her you wouldn't . . .

As the cold light of dawn filters through my window, dog-tired, I can't take any more. I switch off the computer and my phone and lie down on my bed, curling up automatically into a foetal position. And then for the first time in days, miraculously, I sleep.

I don't wake up till nearly midday. My head is clear. Off-loading to my Samaritan has unblocked the toxic waste that has been bunging it up for weeks, and I can think again.

I switch my phone back on and immediately it rings. It's Logan and he's angry.

'Don't you switch your phone off on me!'

I say nothing and this makes him worse.

'Where are you?'

'At home.'

'You got that money ready for me?'

'No.'

'Then you listen to me.' His voice is cold, mean, vicious, like the point of a knife. All pretence of friendliness has gone. 'There's nothing I can do for you if you don't pay. My boss, he's got ways of dealing with little girls like you who won't do as they're told.'

Do I believe him? Is he acting on his own or is he part of some mafia? My body breaks out in a cold sweat and I know I can't afford to take the risk.

'What d'you want?'

'Cash. But if you can't get that, I'll take a credit card. For security. Know what I mean?'

'Yes,' I say, though I don't. 'Where shall I meet you?'

Silence. Then he says, 'Stay put. And keep that phone on. I'll send Scarlett round.'

Scarlett. The person who'd led me to Logan in the first

place. She'd got me into this mess. I could kill her!

I'd trusted Logan because *she'd* vouched for him. She'd told me she'd borrowed money from him when she first arrived, sworn he helped her get off the streets. He was a good guy according to her. He'd seemed like a good guy to me too.

So why had he changed? Why was he acting like this to me?

The penny drops. Because Scarlett was with him now, obviously, and she was angry. She'd gone to him when she left here, of course she had. Who else could she go to? And now she was using him to get her own back at me for chucking her out. 'Cause that's how she saw it. No shades of feeling with Scarlett, only black and white. I was her friend but I'd let her down like everyone else. This was revenge, pure and simple.

Maybe my Samaritan was wrong. Maybe Logan wasn't a loan shark after all. Just someone who was stupidly loyal to Scarlett.

I needed to speak to her. She was the key to all this.

I try her phone but it's switched off, so I ring Rick to see what he thinks, but there's no answer. Finally I manage to contact Mel who says Rick's not at college and where the hell am I?

I feel like I'm going round in circles and getting

nowhere. In the end I decide to head over to Rick's to see if he's there and keep him abreast of the latest developments. I know Logan told me to stay at home but I'll go mad if I don't do something. So I head for his place and before long I'm turning the corner into Bradford Road.

Then, like a giant hand has pulled me back by the scruff of the neck, I leap back round the corner out of sight.

Logan is coming out of Rick's house.

I look again. It's him all right. Same height, same hard face like it's been carved out of granite, same long-limbed swagger. He stops to light up a cigarette. But, the thing is, he's dressed differently. Gone is the street uniform, jeans, hoody, beanie, trainers. In their place are a shaved head, trousers, open-necked shirt, leather jacket. He gets in a car and drives off and I run down the street to Rick's and hammer on the front door. When he opens it he looks relieved to see it's only me.

'What did he want?' I ask.

'Scott?' he says bleakly. 'What he always wants – money. He's coming back this evening for it.'

41

'Scott?'

I can't believe it. Scott is Logan. Or Logan is Scott. Whichever way you want to look at it.

It takes us a while to get our heads around it. Scott, the guy who stole Rick's car off him, triggering the whole torrid chain of events that led us to this point in time, and Logan, the guy I've been borrowing huge sums of money from to get rid of him, are one and the same person.

'But Scarlett knew Logan. She introduced me to him,' I say, baffled.

'Yeah. And Scarlett was with me in the pub the night I met Scott.'

'So,' I say slowly, 'she knows that they're the same person.'

'She set us up! The bitch!'

Rick's eyes narrow as he recalls what happened. 'It was her idea for us to go to the pub in the first place. "Let's go and meet Indie from work," she said. "Give her a surprise."'

'She gave me a bloody surprise all right,' I say bitterly, but Rick ignores me as he recounts what happened that night.

'She was talking at the top of her voice, trying to persuade me to do you a favour and sell the Triumph to pay my fine. Then – surprise, surprise! This guy Scott – or whatever his name is – overhears us and makes me an offer.'

'So he throws in the Chevvie to clinch the deal – which just happens to be stolen – writes you a dud cheque and makes off with the Triumph.'

Rick groans. 'I can't believe I played straight into their hands. And I made it worse! That would've been the end of it if I hadn't seen him driving it a few days later and chased him.'

'Yeah,' I say uncertainly. 'But now when you think about it, that was weird too. Appearing out of nowhere, right in front of your house. It's a bit of a coincidence.'

'What are you saying? He was lying in wait for me?'

'Yep. I think the whole thing was a set-up. Can't you see? He wanted you to chase him.'

Understanding dawns on Rick's face. 'Shit! He made

that crash happen! Shunting, they call it. It's an insurance scam. Car in front stops suddenly and the car behind drives straight into it. Then the first car claims on the other guy's insurance.'

'But in your case, you didn't have insurance. You didn't even have a licence. And Scarlett knew that.'

'So instead he blackmails me. Very clever.'

A look of grudging admiration appears on my boyfriend's face and I yell, 'Rick! He could've killed you.'

'But I still don't get it,' he puzzles. 'He couldn't have been hanging round outside my house twenty-four/seven waiting for me to appear. Someone would've seen him.'

'He didn't have to,' I say bitterly. 'Scarlett tipped him off where we were that night. She phoned me, remember, to see where I was? I told her I was at your place.'

'Cunning bitch! I knew it! It's her we've got to thank for all this,' says Rick bitterly.

He was right. It all made sense now. Niggling things I hadn't even consciously been aware of surfaced. Like, the first time Scarlett introduced me to Logan. I remember now he said he hadn't seen her for months, he'd commented on her new look. But he'd called her Scarlett! He should've called her Suzie, the name she'd discarded along with her old identity.

Why didn't I realize that at the time? Now I come to

think of it, he'd known too much all along. Little slippages in his story – and Scarlett's too – that I should've picked up on if only I'd been more aware. Like the way he always had the money ready and waiting for me.

'It was all Scarlett's fault,' says Rick slowly. 'I knew she was bad news the first time I laid eyes on her. I should have trusted my instincts.'

I fall silent.

'One good thing,' says Rick. 'At least we know now they're acting on their own.'

'How do you know that?'

'They have to be if he's doubling up, playing the crash victim and the loan shark. That makes me feel a whole lot better.'

'What about the blacked-out car?'

'Did you see it?'

'No, but—'

'Scarlett made it up. Like she made everything else up.'

'But why? Why would she do this to us?'

'She never liked me. But you, you were good to her.' He shrugs. 'She's an evil bitch.'

'No,' I say slowly. 'It's not her. It's Scott . . . Logan – whatever his name is. He made her do it.' I hated Scarlett for what she had done to us, I really did. But I couldn't banish the vision in my mind of little Suzie Grey abandoned by her mother, in and out of care, left to fend for herself until she fell into the clutches of a bully who made her do his bidding. 'He's Scarlett's boyfriend. He's been terrorizing her for years.'

'How do you know that?'

'She told me. She came down here to get away from him. I think she genuinely intended to begin a new life as far away from him as possible. But he caught up with her, didn't he? That's when all this trouble began. It's not her, Rick. It's him.'

Rick groans loudly. 'Indie, you are such a sucker for a bad-luck story! You don't have to believe everything she tells you.'

'But it's true!'

'It's not true! She was poison from the beginning. She tried to split us up! She accused me of stealing from your bank account long before he appeared on the scene, in case you've forgotten!'

'She was jealous, that's all!'

'So who stole that money then, Indie? Tell me that!'

I bite my lip as Rick studies me, frustration written all over his face.

'Isn't it obvious? Open your eyes, Indie. Her brute of a boyfriend wasn't even around then.'

'He could've been. I know she must have stolen it but he could have been in the background, pulling her strings.'

Rick explodes. 'That girl stole your life, Scarlett! She stole your job, your money, your peace of mind and she tried to split us up and you're still defending her!' He glares at me. 'You know the worst thing about all this?'

I shake my head.

'You know exactly what she did. But you're still letting her come between us!'

He's right and I admit it and so he calms down. I say no more about her, though inside I'm still convinced that Scarlett is in some ways as much a victim in all this as I am.

Now we know the truth, I can walk away from this nightmare world I fell into. Whereas Scarlett will always remain trapped down the rabbit-hole in a dark, despicable place so long as that mean dog of a boyfriend is waiting to grab her each time she surfaces.

And though Rick doesn't want to hear it, I can't help feeling sorry for her.

'So, what do we do now then?' I sigh. 'Go to the police?'

'I don't know,' he says slowly. 'I'd rather keep them out of it. At the end of the day I was still driving with no licence or insurance. But I don't want them to walk away from this scot-free.'

'Ha-ha,' I say bleakly. '*Scott*-free.'

Rick ignores my pathetic attempt at humour. 'We need to think this through. Scarlett stole money out of your account. I don't know how we're going to get that back.'

'Plus I still owe Logan seven grand.'

This time it's Rick's turn to laugh wryly.

'No you don't. You don't owe him a penny. You were borrowing money from Logan to give me to pay off Scott. But it was all a scam. Between us we were borrowing money from the son of a bitch and handing it straight back to him.'

'I know that, stupid! But he doesn't. He'll still be expecting his money. He's sending Scarlett round to collect.'

'Good. Can't wait to tell her we've worked out her sordid little scheme! And then we can finally get shot of her.'

'No,' I say thoughtfully. 'Leave this to me, Rick. Let me handle Scarlett.'

'Indie!' he says warningly. 'You're too soft. Don't you dare let her get away with it.'

Rick knows me like the back of his hand. Or he thinks he does. Despite all that she'd done to me, I still wasn't prepared to think the worst of Scarlett. We were all capable of acting badly, the events of the last few weeks had taught me that. I'd taken money myself, from my sister and my employer, even though it was with the best of intentions. So what chance did someone like Scarlett have?

But Rick knew nothing about that. No one did.

I make up my mind. I'm going to come clean and have it out with her. And then I'm going to give her the opportunity to put things right.

One last chance. For her. And for me.

'I won't,' I say and kiss him goodbye. Then I go back home to wait for Scarlett.

42

I haven't been at home long before the house phone rings. I answer it expecting to hear Logan's voice, but to my surprise, it's Shazza.

'Indie?' she says. 'How are you?'

'Fine. You?'

'It's all kicking off here,' she says, her voice wobbling with excitement. 'Is Scarlett there?'

'No. She moved out some time ago.'

'D'you know where she is?'

I hesitate. 'No. Why?'

'I knew it!' she squeaks triumphantly. 'She's done a runner. She hasn't been in for days.'

'I'm sorry, I can't help . . .'

'Only there's money missing from the till.'

'How much?'

'About eighty quid.'

My heart starts beating like a bass drum. 'Who do they think it is?'

'Her, of course.'

'Why?'

''Cos she was cashing up every night. And now she's gone. Stands to reason, don't it? I never liked her, two-faced cow. She dropped you in it loads.'

'Me?' I say, startled.

'Yeah. Said you couldn't be arsed to come in. Rather spend time with your fella. I knew she was lying.'

'Did she say that to Gordon?'

'Yeah, loads of times. Oops, got to go, Indi love. Hurry up and come back. I miss you!'

As I put the phone down I hear a key inserted into the front door. I walk out into the hall to see Scarlett standing there looking guarded.

'Anyone at home?'

'Just me. You'd better come upstairs.'

When she walks past her old room, Tam's, Scarlett barely gives it a second glance, but when she enters mine she looks around it like she did the first time and says sourly, 'You don't know how bloody lucky you are, living in a place like this.'

'Yes I do,' I say shortly. Then I add, 'What are you

doing here, Scarlett?'

She looks surprised. 'I've come for Logan's money.'

'I haven't got it,' I say. 'You know I can't lay my hands on that amount.'

She shrugs. 'Can't help you there.'

'You've bled me dry.'

'Nothing to do with me, Indie. This is an arrangement you made with Logan, not me. I was only trying to help you out.'

'Are you working for him?'

'Nope. I've come to collect the money you owe him, that's all,' she says coolly. 'Any objections?'

'Yes! You should be ashamed of yourself, Scarlett. Running round doing his dirty work for him.'

'I can do what I like!'

'But you're not, are you? Doing what you like? You're doing what he tells you to.'

'I don't do what any bloke tells me. I do what I want.'

'Stop lying! I know all about him, Scarlett.'

She looks wary. 'I don't know what you're on about.'

'I know who he is. Logan.'

She's completely still, a startled deer caught in the headlights, waiting. I mustn't frighten her or she could bolt. One slow step at a time.

'He's your boyfriend, isn't he?'

Her eyes widen.

'The one you ran away from?'

She gives a little laugh. 'So?'

'Don't do it,' I plead. 'Don't drag me into this.'

'Why should I care about you? You chucked me out!'

'We can go to the police and tell them what he's like. Tell them he makes you do stuff you don't want,' I say desperately. 'Tell them he's a loan shark.'

'Why would I do that?' Her face is hard.

'Because he's controlling you!'

'Because you're in deep shit and you can't pay him back the money you owe him, you mean!'

'That's true!' I am determined to get her to escape his clutches. 'But you could be free of him if you want to be. We don't have to get the police involved. You could just walk away.'

She studies me, eyes full of contempt. 'And what if I don't want to?'

'I'm offering you a chance, Scarlett. I want to help you live your own life.'

'I do live my own life, you silly bitch!' she snaps. 'One I choose, not you.'

Then she laughs out loud, sneering, proud, boastful.

'You don't get it, do you? Nobody tells me what to do,

not you, not Logan, not anyone. There's only one person who runs my life and that's me.'

And suddenly I know, without a shadow of a doubt, that she is telling the truth.

43

Over the past three months I have been:

Lied to.

Stolen from.

Humiliated.

Betrayed.

Manipulated.

Threatened.

Set up.

Brought down.

Scammed.

Shafted.

I'd been subjected to this by a vicious, greedy parasite who had preyed on me, crawling all over me, sucking me dry, rendering me helpless and stupid with terror.

Scarlett walked into my world and stole my life.

Nobody made her. Nobody forced her. She looked around carefully and selected me, like a dress off a rack, and tried on my life. It suited her. For now. I was this season's hot choice. So she helped herself to it, just like she grabbed whatever she wanted on a shoplifting spree.

And I'd allowed her to do this. I'd made it so easy for her. She's watching me now, cunning as ever.

'A word of warning. You're up to here in it, Indie. You don't want to mess with this Scott character. You've no idea what blokes like him will do.'

She's loving this, you can tell. Scarlett, the puller of strings, the supreme puppeteer who makes everybody dance to her tune.

'You need guys like Logan, whether you like it or not. You'd be in deep trouble if you didn't pay Scott back. You and that pretty boyfriend of yours.'

She's piling it on, trying to scare me. She's pitiless. I never realized she hated me so much.

Yet, bizarrely I am pretty sure this is not personal. It can't be. She's done it before, it's obvious. She's a professional. She'd selected me because I was an easy target. Indie, the girl with the big heart, the collector of waifs and strays. What a soft touch.

And there'd be more soft touches like me. She was about to move on, I was pretty sure of it. She'd left her job at the salon, hadn't been to college. Her time here was nearly up. Time to leech on to some other poor sucker.

And Logan – or Scott – or whatever his name was. Names didn't seem to be that important. When your identity is shifting, any name will do. He'd go with her. They were a team. He was the brawn but she was the brains. She was in charge.

Well, I might be a soft touch, but I had brains too. And in this cheating, lying, deceitful game she had forced me to play against my will, I held a trump card. She had no idea I knew that Scott and Logan were the same person.

I take a deep breath. I know what I have to do.

'I've no money. But Logan said he'd take a credit card instead.'

'Have you got one?'

'My dad has. Downstairs. I'll go and get it.'

Her eyes widen in surprise. She didn't expect me to be such a pushover.

I run downstairs to the lounge and pull out Dad's credit-card holder from his desk, selecting the one he keeps for holidays. I scribble down the PIN number from the book he keeps all his PINs and passwords in, security not being my dad's forté. I leave it open on top of the desk and go back upstairs and hand the card to her.

'PIN number?'

I pass it to her without a word.

'How do I know this'll work?'

'Try it at a cash-machine if you want. I'll come with you, make sure it's OK.'

She nods and stands up to go. 'Scarlett?' I say suddenly, my voice wretched. 'What would it take to pay off someone like Scott once and for all?'

She comes to a stop and looks at me, wondering where this is going.

'A thousand? Two? Tell me! I can't take this any more. I just want to be rid of him for good.'

Her face is greedy, calculating. 'Dunno. Three maybe? Three thou should do it.'

'Do you think Logan would lend me that much? I haven't got any money at the moment but he can have some other stuff for security till I can pay him off.'

'Like what?'

'Um. More credit cards? Passports? Driving licences? Look!' I rush to my dressing table and scrabble through my top drawer till I find my own passport and thrust it into her hands. 'Take this for now. Ask Logan for three grand. I can get you some more, I promise.'

'OK. That's ten grand you owe us now.' I notice the 'us'. If I wanted any more proof, this was it. 'A nice round number,' she adds with satisfaction, slipping the passport quickly into her bag as if she's afraid I'll change my mind.

'Scott's coming tonight for the money,' I say, my voice broken. 'Can you get it to me before then?'

'Shouldn't be a problem.'

Downstairs the front door opens and Mum calls, 'Anyone in?' Perfect timing.

'Come on,' I say to Scarlett. 'It's time to go.'

Mum is surprised to see Scarlett coming down the stairs after me. Her mouth purses up. 'Hello,' she says coldly and then goes into the lounge and shuts the door. When we go outside, Scarlett is really put out.

'Don't know what I ever did to upset her,' she says annoyed. 'Snotty cow!'

I stifle my anger and don't enlighten her. We make our way to the high street and the nearest cash-machine. As we approach it I suddenly come to a stop.

'I can't do this! I can't steal my dad's money.'

She looks alarmed. 'You can't back out now. And if you want to borrow some more, then you've got to show you can meet the repayments.'

'OK,' I say, backing away. 'You've got the PIN number. But don't ask me to watch.'

She gives a sly grin and says, 'Suits me,' and heads off to the cash-machine on her own. I turn away. A couple of minutes later she's back, looking a bit disgruntled.

'It would only let me have two hundred and fifty quid,' she grumbles and I knew she was trying to take out the thousand in one go. I feel sick. *Hold your nerve, Indie. You can do this.*

'You can take more out tomorrow,' I say. 'My dad's not going to miss it for a while. That card's the one we use for holidays.'

'Right then,' she says, 'I'm going to take this back to Logan and tell him how much you want. I'll call you later.'

'Thanks Scarlett,' I say humbly. 'I don't know what I'd do without you.'

I insert my key in the lock and the door swings open. My mother is there with hands on her hips and a face full of fury.

'I thought I told you that girl was no longer welcome in this house!'

'She's not! I came home to find her here alone! She was in the lounge. I didn't ask her to come.'

'I knew it!'

'What's happened?

'When I walked in here the desk was open and so was this bloody book of your father's with all his passwords in it. She'd been going through our things.'

'No!' My face registers shock. 'She hasn't pinched anything, has she?'

'I can't be sure. Your father's credit-card holder is here but I can't tell if anything is missing from it till he comes home. Oh Indigo,' she says fretfully, 'I wish you'd be a bit more careful about who you invite into our home.'

'I will be from now on,' I say with feeling.

'How did she get in, that's what I want to know?' I look embarrassed. 'Indie, she doesn't still have a key, does she?'

'I'll get it back from her,' I mutter. 'I don't want anything more to do with her.'

'I should think not!' says Mum. 'I'll call the police if she comes round again, bothering us. Little thief! I should've listened to your father and reported her when she stole that money from Tamsyn's bag. I don't feel safe in my bed with people like her around.'

I go upstairs to my room, looking suitably chastened. Then I phone Rick and keep him up to speed. When he hears about the extra three grand I've asked for he gasps, 'Shit, Indie! I hope you know what you're doing!'

'So do I,' I mutter. We discuss the next part of my plan. Then I sit down and wait till Scarlett calls.

44

It doesn't take them long to lay their hands on three grand. How many people could do that? I get a sour taste in my mouth when I think how many times she played the poverty trick on me. When she rings I slip out and meet her round the corner. I don't want her turning up at my house again. Yet.

She takes out the envelope but hangs on to it. 'You got more credit cards for me?'

I shake my head. 'Not yet. Sorry. You can have them first thing tomorrow morning.'

She looks at me with a trace of suspicion and I say defensively, 'My mum's home, isn't she? You know what she's like. She's got eyes in the back of her head. I'll have to wait till tonight when she's asleep.'

She sniffs and holds on to the envelope teasingly,

enjoying the power she holds over me. I fight down the urge to slap her. That money would be passing from her hands to mine to Rick's to Scott's and straight back to hers in the course of a couple of hours. As far as she was concerned, it was safe. But still she couldn't resist tormenting me.

'Please, Scarlett,' I plead. 'Rick needs that money to pay Scott off. You don't know what he's like. He scares us both to death.'

'Make sure your boyfriend gets it safely to him,' she says finally and hands me the envelope. 'There's three grand in there. Be careful, Indie. There are a lot of thieves about.'

Oh Scarlett. Or Suzie. Or whoever you are. This is just a game to you, isn't it? A taunting, sadistic, torturous, vindictive game played to your rules which only you can win. You love it all, don't you? Setting the trap, luring your victims in, holding them captive, pinning them down, watching them squirm. Tricking and duping and cheating and snaring your way through life, you think you're so clever. You think no one is a match for you.

I am about to prove you wrong.

I slip back into the house without Mum even noticing I'd gone. As soon as Dad comes home she tells him Scarlett had been in the house alone. He discovers the password book open and one of his cards missing.

'I knew it!' says Mum. 'It's that blasted girl.'

'I'm sorry,' I groan. 'I should never have asked her to stay.'

'It's not your fault. She fooled us all.'

'Better cancel your card, Dad,' I say, trying to be helpful.

'Good point.' He picks up the phone and wanders off. Soon he's back again, looking grim.

'Too late. There's already been a withdrawal. This afternoon on the high street.'

'That's it,' she says grimly. 'I'm calling the police.'

When the bell goes five minutes later Mum says, 'That was quick.' But it's Rick looking suitably fed up.

'What's up?'

'My car's been nicked.'

'Your Triumph Herald?' says Dad. 'You're joking!'

'I wish I was. I haven't even finished paying for it.'

'Have you told the police?' Dad asks.

'Not yet.' He looks a bit sheepish. 'I wanted to tell Indie first.'

Mum puts her arm round him. 'Well you can save yourself a phone call, love, they're on their way.' She tells him what's happened and he looks suitably shocked.

'I never trusted that Scarlett,' he says somewhat truthfully. He starts telling a tale about money disappearing from bags at college and he doesn't even say it was her but Mum jumps to predictable conclusions. So she tells him how it's not the first time it's happened, money had been taken from Tamsyn's bag, and then I chip in with the conversation I'd had with Shazza earlier on about money disappearing from the salon.

The power of suggestion. It is so easy to tear someone's reputation to shreds . . .

By the time two police officers arrive, Scarlett has been hung, drawn and quartered by my mother and the bits have been hung out to dry. I relate to them how I came home that afternoon to find her in the house on her own. I don't need to say anything else, Mum takes over then and fills them in on the rest. They ask if anything else is missing and I go upstairs to check. After a suitable period I come downstairs distressed. My passport has gone.

They ask questions, take notes, wanting to find out everything they can about Scarlett. 'It's not her real name,' I explain. 'She just called herself that. Her real name is Suzie Grey.' They exchange looks, then do a search. There are thousands of Suzie Greys.

'Probably not her real name either,' one says.

They want more information but I have no more to give.

'I took her in, I looked after her because she didn't have anyone. I thought she was my friend. Now I don't know who she is or where she is and that's the truth.' Then I add for good measure, 'I wish I did. I'm worried about her.'

Mum raises her eyes to heaven. 'What am I going to do with her? Will she never learn?'

'Don't you worry, Indigo. I would say Miss Suzie Grey is very capable of looking after herself,' says one of the officers. 'We'll get back to you as soon as we've got some news.'

When they've gone Rick and I go upstairs and switch our phones back on.

'I think Scott's been trying to get hold of me,' says Rick, a ghost of that old familiar smile appearing on his face. 'What a shame! I believe I might have missed an appointment with him.'

'Oh look! I think Scarlett might want to speak to me too.'

Our in-boxes are chock-full of messages.

Everything going according to plan. Our faces break into big smiles as we switch our phones back off and settle down to wait.

45

Later on, Mum comes upstairs and knocks lightly on my door. 'We're off to bed, Indie, it's been quite a night.' Rick scrambles to his feet but she says, 'No, no, you don't have to leave till you're ready.'

'I won't be long,' he says.

Dad appears behind her. 'Sorry about your car, Rick. We've been thinking. Do you reckon that could have had anything to do with Scarlett too?'

Bingo!

'Dunno. That hadn't occurred to me. You might have a point there,' says Rick.

'Oh well,' sighs Mum. 'I expect we'll find out sooner or later. In the meantime I think we could all do with a good night's sleep!'

'Goodnight!' we chorus, then, as they close the door

behind them, we grin at each other.

'That's a first!' whispers Rick. 'Going to bed and leaving me alone with their daughter in her bedroom. Anything could happen!'

'I think they finally trust you,' I whisper back. 'Everything's relative. Compared to Scarlett you're a saint.'

Then our faces become serious.

'Ready?' he asks.

I take a deep breath. 'Ready.' I switch my phone back on and call Scarlett.

'I've been trying to ring you all night!' she says angrily.

'Sorry! Been trying to catch up with work. I'm so behind! It's hard to concentrate . . .'

'Where's Rick?'

'Rick? At home as far as I know. Why?'

There's a pause. Then she says, 'Logan wants to speak to him.'

'Logan? What about?'

'He's not happy about lending you that three grand. It's too much, he says. He wants it back.'

'Why?'

'I dunno! He's had second thoughts.'

'But I haven't got it. I gave it to Rick . . .'

'So what's he bloody well done with it?'

'Given it to Scott I suppose!' My voice rises in distress. 'What's going on, Scarlett?'

'That's what I want to know,' she says grimly. 'Hang on a minute.' It's blatantly obvious to me she's talking to Logan because she comes back on and says decisively, 'We're coming round, Indie. We need to sort this out.'

'Now?' I say in alarm. 'Can't it wait? My parents are in bed. You'll disturb them. They'll hear the doorbell—'

'I've got a key, I'll let myself in,' she says and hangs up.

I turn to Rick and thrust a clenched fist into the air.

'Result!'

The house is still and hushed but alert, like an animal in the darkness waiting to catch its prey. Rick is lying on his back on my bed, staring at the ceiling, his arms crossed behind his head. I'm sitting still as a statue on the top step of the narrow flight of stairs that leads up to my room. Below me I can see a strip of light beneath my parents' door. I thought Scarlett and Logan would be here by now. I check my watch but it's too dark to make out the time. I should be scared but I'm not.

Last night I sat in the darkness and talked to a stranger.

Tonight I'm a cat poised to pounce.

I raise my head, listening. A key in the lock. A door opening downstairs. I stand up. Rick is behind me, he's heard it too. He nods and I slip downstairs, my bare feet soundless as I pad past my parents' bedroom. From there I can just make out Logan's outline and Scarlett's pale face staring up at me. I tiptoe down to join them.

'In here,' I whisper and we go in the lounge. My hand moves to the light switch but Logan says, 'No!' and closes the door behind us.

'What do you want?' I ask.

'The money back,' he says.

'I haven't got it. I gave it to Rick.'

'I want the money.' He pushes his face so close to mine I can smell his breath and I find myself cringing.

'I haven't got it,' I repeat, my voice little more than a whisper, and I look round desperately. 'I can give you more credit cards. Passports. Anything! It's all in here.'

'They'll do, Logan,' snaps Scarlett. 'Till tomorrow.'

Logan takes his face out of mine. I was right. He's the brute but she's the brains behind all this. I open my dad's desk and start rummaging through it. It's hard to see, the only light is from the street-light outside, and I'm nervous, dropping things on the floor.

'Hurry up!' she says impatiently so I say, 'Give me your bag,' and scoop a pile of documents straight into it. Logan is behind me. I can feel his breath on my neck. He's nervous too, they both are, I can feel it. So am I. I'm nearly there. Where's Rick? Where's Rick when I need him?

Suddenly the door crashes opens and the light is switched on. Rick is standing there staring at us, Scarlett, Logan and me, the bag in my hand.

'Scott?' he says pleasantly. 'What are you doing here?'

Then he opens his mouth and yells at the top of his voice. 'Help! Police! Burglars! Get the police!'

We did it!

46

They got away. I'm glad. We could have stopped them if we'd wanted but that wasn't part of the plan. It wasn't Scarlett I needed, it was her bag. Crammed full of evidence.

Five assorted credit and debit cards and – Yes! Bonus! – one previously stolen credit card. Dad's.

Two driving licences. Mum's and Dad's.

Three passports. Mum's, Dad's and – Yes! Second bonus! – mine, still there from Scarlett's previous visit this afternoon.

Various account details I'd scooped into the bag along with the above.

One house key belonging to us.

Plus a wallet containing a fair bit of cash, odd bits of make-up and a hairbrush.

'No phone,' says the officer I hand it over to. 'That's a shame. We can trace quite a lot nowadays through a mobile.'

I knew that. That's why I'd dived into the bag and retrieved it, stuffing it in my back pocket when my parents chased outside with Rick to catch them. They were too late. They'd gone.

Logan's survival instinct had kicked in fast. No fight, just flight for him, straight out through the front door. Not Scarlett. She stood her ground, tried to snatch her bag back, but we were too fast for her. I threw it out of her reach as Rick grabbed her from behind. She was struggling, desperate, we could hear Mum's voice, high, urgent, calling the police. 'Go!' I hissed. 'Just go!' Her eyes widened then Rick threw her into the hall, where she took one look at Mum and Dad and dived out the front door.

A matter of seconds and it was all over.

The next day the police complete their investigation. They study the CCTV camera at the cashpoint in the high street which shows Scarlett, bold as brass, withdrawing money on my dad's card. They talk to Gordon at Herr Cutz who confirms that eighty quid went missing during the period when Scarlett was cashing up for him. They take a statement from Tamsyn in which she claims categorically that Scarlett stole money from her handbag. They talk to Rick, whose car has been stolen, and indicate they think that it's highly likely that Scarlett's boyfriend is the culprit. They are helpful, telling him to inform the finance company, giving him a special number so he doesn't get into trouble.

The police have been very sympathetic. Scarlett's and Logan's descriptions have been circulated around other forces. They are not looking for anyone else in relation to this crime.

47

Scammers scammed.

Shafters shafted.

We conned that last three thousand pounds out of them for the repayments on Rick's car. But in the end he didn't have to pay back the finance company after all.

We are quids in. Three thousand of them.

Rick wants to buy a new car. Unsurprisingly, I say no.

'You haven't even got a licence,' I remind him.

'How about a gap year then, when we've finished our courses? Australia? Thailand? India?'

It's very tempting. But I can't. I've got debts to pay.

Nobody will let me though. Not Dad, not Gordon, not even Tamsyn.

'It wasn't your fault,' they all say and then I feel bad. I insist I feel responsible but they won't hear of it.

'When are you coming back, Indie?' asks Gordon. 'I'm sorry I listened to Scarlett and her lies. She completely fooled me, that girl.'

'Me too,' I say regretfully.

He puts his arm round my shoulders and gives me a squeeze. 'Older and wiser, hey?'

I am older and wiser, yes. It could all have ended so differently. But I'm sadder too. Because now I know there are thousands of people out there trapped in a cycle of debt, fearful for their safety.

I'm sad as well because I've lost my faith in others. And I've lost my belief in myself.

I don't know how much of what Scarlett or rather Suzie – or whatever her real name is – told me was true. I don't know if she really was neglected, or worse, as a child or if she was brought up in care or not. She could've made it up for all I know. I definitely don't believe her story about escaping an abusive boyfriend any more. Scarlett was no victim of Logan's, that's for sure. She was in charge.

But despite what everyone says, I still wonder how much of this was my fault. Did Scarlett recognize me as a soft touch and target me from the start? Or did she really think of me as a friend and only got nasty when I accused her of stealing from my account? Which, let's face it, she must have done.

I'll never know.

Strangely, I am not really worried about revenge. Scarlett and Logan have lost their threat. I think they were scheming rather than evil and now they'll cut their losses and move on. Like the police said, it won't be the first time they've done this and it certainly won't be the last. It's how they make their living, moving around from place to place, looking for gullible people like me to prey on.

For *gullible* people read *good*.

But I don't feel good any more.

The money is in the bottom of my wardrobe, still in its envelope, curled up in the toe of an old pair of boots. I don't want it there. It doesn't belong to me. It pollutes the air that I breathe, it taints my bedroom, especially at night as I try to sleep. It's dirty. It stinks.

I can't sleep. Earlier tonight Rick and I went to the Christmas Ball. We didn't win the Hottest Couple this year. We're different people now. When your life has crashed around you, you're bound to be left with a few scars.

I turn over and thump my pillow, wishing I could get to sleep. When I was a kid I could never sleep at Christmas, I was too excited. Back then I used to think everyone was happy at Christmas time. How naïve was that? I didn't know about the sad, the bad, the frightened, the lonely, the suicidal.

My mind flips back to the night I sat in the darkness and talked to a stranger who saved my life.

I reach for my phone.

'Samaritans. Can I help you?'

'I'd like to speak to Mrs Moffat please.'

Pause.

'I'm sorry, we have nobody here of that name. Can I help?'

'Yes,' I say, smiling to myself. What did I expect, her sitting there, waiting for my call? 'Can you tell me where my local branch is?' I give my address.

I get up and dress, tucking the envelope from my boots into my coat pocket. Outside it's cold, damp, murky. It doesn't feel like Christmas. It should be clear and frosty for Santa to find his way.

I walk quickly, straight down the deserted high street. Not quite deserted. In the doorway of the chemist, a down-and-out sleeps in his coat, huddled in filthy blankets, empty bottle by his side. I slip five twenty-pound notes out of the envelope and tuck them inside his coat then hurry on. He'll think Christmas has come for him after all.

At the end of the road a light from a room above an

empty shop struggles to penetrate the mist. I've reached my destination. I try the door but it's shut. I press the intercom and a voice says, 'Samaritans. Can I help?'

'I need to speak to someone,' I say and the door clicks open. I run up the narrow stairs. Another door. I push it and enter.

A man is sitting behind a desk. He looks up.

'Can I help you?' he asks.

I glance around. A woman is talking on the phone at the desk next to him; another is sitting at a computer. One is old, one is young. Neither of them look like Mrs Moffat.

It doesn't matter.

'Did you want someone to talk to?' he asks.

'Not any more,' I say. 'I'm all right now. But I want you to have this.'

I slide the envelope across the desk to him. He peers inside then looks up at me in shock.

'What's it for?' he asks.

'For listening,' I say.

Then I walk away.

SCARLETT

In the ladies' loos at Victoria Station I splash my face with cold water then stare glumly at my reflection in the mirror.

Not looking my best, am I? Got spoilt living with Indie, that's my trouble. Haircuts, makeovers, nice clothes, money to spend. I was doing all right till I got greedy.

Now I'm stuck with Steve, aka Logan. He's still kicking off because Rick and Indie got one over on him. I've come in here to get away from the sound of his voice, playing the same busted tune over and over again like a broken record.

'That was my money! He owes me three grand! He's not going to get away with it, no way! I'm going back to find the little tyke and break every bone in his body!'

Actually, he said quite a lot more than that. I've left out

359

all the effing and blinding. Everyone was looking at him, giving him a wide berth.

I wish he'd give it a rest. We can't go back, he knows that. We'd be picked up by the police straight away.

I sigh heavily. You win some, you lose some, get over it. It was Steve's money so, to tell the truth, I don't give a shit.

'Are you OK?'

A girl is standing behind me, staring at me in the mirror, her eyes brimming with concern. A lumpy girl with shoulder-length hair wearing a long scarf, a loose, shapeless jumper and faded jeans. Student-type. Caring. My heart leaps.

'Not really,' I say with a choked little sob. It never fails. Instantly she looks worried.

'Only I couldn't help overhearing that guy outside . . .'

I stare down at the basin feigning embarrassment.

'Is he your boyfriend?' She's nibbling at the bait, cod-eyed with curiosity.

I nod like I'm too upset to speak but inside I feel a sharp tug of excitement.

'Is anything wrong?'

'He's just angry . . .' My voice trails away.

'You don't have to put up with that, you know,' she says, her round face practically quivering with indignation.

I say nothing, allowing her imagination to fill in the silence.

'Look,' she says hesitantly, 'd'you want to talk?'

I peer nervously over my shoulder as if I'm afraid he's going to walk in on us. 'I can't,' I mumble. 'He won't let me.'

Instantly she's hooked.

'Hang on.' Bristling, she marches to the door and looks out at the busy concourse. 'He's not watching out for you, he's on his mobile,' she says and I give her a helpless, watery little smile and finally reel her in. 'Come on!' she says urgently. 'My place is just around the corner. I'll make you a coffee and you can tell me all about it.'

How simple was that and I wasn't even trying? Do I want this fish?

I take a quick peek at Steve as we exit the toilets. He's stopped ranting and raving at last and is lost in a world of his own, playing on his phone, his mouth slack.

What have I got to lose? Time to move on. I was better off working on my own anyway.

'What's your name?' she asks as we leave the station. I peer up at the shop we are passing. Claire's Accessories.

'Claire,' I whisper. 'Claire Brown. What's yours?'

'Lowenna.'

'Lowenna? That's a nice name.'

'Thanks.' She smiles and squeezes my arm.

Caught. And landed.